Shadows of the Mind

This piece focuses on teenage rape, pregnancy, schizophrenia and alcoholism within a family's household.

You know the saying — "There's one in every family" be it an alcoholic, or schizophrenic — there's one in every family. Although in larger families, there is usually more than one.

Shadows of the Mind brings these issues to a greater vision in the characters depicted in each chapter.

Order this book online at www.trafford.com
or email orders@trafford.com

Most Trafford titles are also available at major online book retailers.

Printed in Victoria, BC, Canada.

ISBN: 978-1-4120-2734-2 (sc)

*Our mission is to efficiently provide the world's finest, most comprehensive book publishing
service, enabling every author to experience success. To find out how to publish your book, your
way, and have it available worldwide, visit us online at www.trafford.com*

Trafford rev. 1/13/2010

 www.trafford.com

North America & international
toll-free: 1 888 232 4444 (USA & Canada)
phone: 250 383 6864 ♦ fax: 812 355 4082

Acknowledgments

"I give thanks to God Almighty for sparing my life. In addition, for giving me the strength and courage to fulfill my dream in completing **_Shadows of the Mind_**.

Six years ago, having various X-Rays, cat scans, a MRA and finally a MRI — I was diagnosed with having a leaking aneurysm that could burst at any moment. After being rushed into emergency surgery and released, I picked up this manuscript and began to write once again. I was unable to write before my surgery due to the excessive pain I endured.

God had spared my life and my life now had purpose. I knew that it was His plan and purpose to have me fulfill my dream of writing."

To Kaisy R. Wilkerson — thank you so much for taking the time out of your busy schedule to review each chapter of my final draft. To my dear friends Lisa Williams and Loretta Coble — thank you both for getting me back on track by editing my ROUGH draft... just because I asked.

To my Family — I love you dearly. For everyone has a story and to each individual esteems his own story.

Pam Randall

Growing up in a family of twelve, seven girls and five boys was adventurous for the Tucker children and quite wearisome for their parents, George and Joyce Tucker.

Grandpa Fred and Grandma Sara, Joyce's parents, settled in the small town of Rocking Barrel after Grandpa Fred's job with the railroad relocated him out of an even smaller town in South Carolina. After the railroad project was complete, Sara and Fred agreed to settle there in Rocking Barrel. It was in this small town that Joyce Tucker, an infant child at the time, was found on Fred and Sara's doorstep.

Grandma Sara, forty-two and Grandpa Fred, a little over eighty, found great joy and delight in keeping Joyce and raising her as their own child.

Quiet whispers swept through Rocking Barrel of how Sara had become pregnant by someone other than Fred and of course, that she had lied about finding her on their doorstep. Fred took good care of Joyce. He loved her deeply... as if she were his own flesh and blood. He ensured that she had the best of everything while he lived and even after his death. Sara and Joyce continued to live on quite comfortably there in Rocking Barrel after Fred died of old age. They benefited from his railroad pension.

4

Chapter 2

Joyce met George in high school and it was love at first sight. He walked her home from school everyday carrying her books across his shoulders. He walked proudly down a long rocky dirt road that stretched onward for over fifteen miles. Although their courtship was hard and strenuous in the days when teenagers were marrying at the ages of fourteen and fifteen, George and Joyce had other plans. Surely they loved one another dearly and yearned to be married as many of their friends were. They knew that their desires had to wait knowing that they wanted to someday raise a family. Joyce and George chose to give their careers first priority.

After graduating from high school, Joyce left Rocking Barrel and attended Shaw University where she received her Bachelors Degree in Science. She then returned to South Carolina where she attended Paine College where she earned her Masters Degree in English Literature. George remained behind in Rocking Barrel where he took on odd jobs to make money. The couple, of course, continued to see one another when Joyce returned home from school during her summer vacations. The bus ride back home was grueling but it was worth it to see her family and George.

Having waited patiently, a nineteen-year-old George wasted no time in asking his high school sweetheart for her hand in marriage in 1942. To his delight, she accepted his proposal and immediately they eloped off to South Carolina where they were married at a small courthouse. Nicholas and Miriam Tucker, George's brother and younger sister, went along to witness the marriage ceremony.

Three months later, in the midst of World War II, George decided to join the United States Army to serve and protect his country.

"I wish you wouldn't join," Joyce pleaded with her husband.

However he knew that he had no other choice but to go and give his support. He was certain that his military position would someday earn him the necessary skills he desired to take care of his wife.

Chapter 3

After serving three years fighting in World War II, George returned back home to the States in 1945. He settled in Rocking Barrel for only a short period when he was given his second tour of duty to Washington, DC. Joyce was not yet prepared to join her sweetheart at his military duty station due to the dropping of the Atomic Bomb. She decided that it was best that she remain behind in Rocking Barrel. She waited anxiously for his return. With each visit, she remained behind with child: Rosetta, Sassy, Victor and Calvin all conceived and born during George's short visits.

In 1953 when George returned home to the States, once again, he was rushed immediately back out of the country to Germany. It was now that Joyce had enough of being away from her husband. She decided that she and the children would join him on this journey.

"Mama, George has been given a tour of duty to Germany and I really would like to go with him this time," she explained to Grandma Sara. "Could you please keep Calvin here with you while I take the other children with us?" she pleaded.

"Sure, I don't see why not," Grandma Sara, agreed.

"You go and be with George. I will be delighted to keep Calvin. When will you be leaving?"

"We have a week before we leave," Joyce told her mother.

"Why have you chosen to leave Calvin behind and not the other children?"

"I don't know... he's only a year old, the youngest. It's going to be hard to manage there in a strange country and even more so if I take all of these children."

"I'm certain you're right. Well go on home and start packing," Grandma Sara said excitedly.

A week later, George and Joyce along with their three children were off to Germany. They left Calvin behind in Rocking Barrel with Grandma Sara.

The family remained in Germany for three more years while Joyce taught English on the base and George continued to serve his country. Sassy, Victor and Rosetta attended school there that first year. The following two years Bobby and Felicia... two additional children arrived on the scene. They remained at home with the Nanny, Auntie Mattie.

"George, do you think that we can go home after this tour? I'm tired of traveling and we need to find some stability for the children's sake."

Joyce had hoped that after serving fourteen years in the military that George would retire. She often expressed her wishes of wanting to return back home to the States.

"Be patient Joyce we will be going home soon," he replied, ignoring Joyce's wishes. He continued to serve in the army and accepted yet another tour, which led them to Maine in early 1956. It was in Maine where Joyce gave birth to Mona and Ginger.

"I dread having to wake up to shivers each morning! It's a hard job having to get up and even more getting these five children off to school. You try dressing them and walking twenty miles with them... it's a struggle George."

Joyce confessed her struggles for the first time to George that August morning.

"Surely after fourteen-years and eight children... you too, must be tired of traveling!"

"I love traveling. You should be glad that I got you out of Rocking Barrel. I don't know why you are in such a hurry to return there. Everything you need is right here with you," he told her as he walked out of the house, ending the conversation.

Joyce continued to teach in Maine for two years, before feeling forced to give up her career. It was cheaper for the family if she stayed home to care for the children instead of paying the

Nanny. Even with the children home with her Joyce felt that her life was wasting away now that she was no longer teaching. She began to drink heavily for the remaining two years that they remained there in Maine.

"It has been eighteen years, George. I believe it is time that we return to Rocking Barrel!" she demanded in a drunken rampage.

"You might as well start to pack... I've already accepted a two-year tour in Washington, DC. We will be leaving in a month," he said.

At a lost for words, Joyce walked slowly away from him. She knew that she was in a no win situation and had no choice but to join him in Washington. Greatly disappointed in his decision, she refused to have any dealings with him for a month. She did as he suggested and began to pack their belongings. At the end of the Washington tour, George had served twenty years in the United States Army. While in Washington, Little-Joyce and Borne, the twins, were conceived during this tour in August of 1960. Joyce continued to stress her desire of wanting to go back home to Rocking Barrel.

"George, it has been twenty years and you have earned a full retirement packet. This should be enough for you to take care of us for the rest of our lives. For the sake of the children and our marriage, let's please go back home."

"Just one more tour Joyce and I promise you I'll retire. I've already accepted a tour in El Paso and I've always wanted to go there; besides, honey, you will love Texas."

The family was off to Texas, away from the chilling weather in Maine. Joyce was displeased with Texas because of the torturing humidity and sweltering heat. After giving birth to Nicholas in the spring of 1962, she had enough of the longhorn state and returned to Rocking Barrel.

"I thought that you were going to retire two years ago. What will be your excuse this time for re-enlisting? I can't take this traveling from town to town with all these children. This is it, I'm going home!" She cried her final words before charging out of the door and leaving him behind in Texas.

George put up no fight as he watched Joyce and his children leave. She returned home to Rocking Barrel with her ten children where she rented a small white house on a corner lot. Not long after they had settled into the home, George decided to come home to visit his family.

"I will be coming home to join you and the children... I promise after this tour," he promised.

A week later, he got on the plane and returned to Texas. He came home to visit during the holidays and sent money home to assist with the bills and food, however it never seemed to be enough.

Chapter 4

The quaint house was a small three-bedroom duplex made up primarily of wood that sat on a cement foundation. It had two front entrances and two doors at its rear side. The house would be described as a split-level duplex apartment. The majority of the homes in Rocking Barrel were built in this design.

Life was extremely hard for the Tuckers during the time that George was fulfilling his military obligations. Joyce was drinking more and more everyday. She was drinking Vodka by the fifth and even during her pregnancy with Kim. After Kim was born on September 11, 1964, George refused to send money home to take care of Joyce and the children. He also stopped coming home to visit. Rumors in Rocking Barrel flew that Kim was not George's child. This initiated his abandonment of his wife and children.

Kim was three, if not four, when she recalled meeting her father for the first time when he chose to journey home. His teeth shined exquisitely, gleaming radiantly like a string of white pearls. She recalled this as he flashed a huge smile once entering through the front door. He stood there dignified in his perfectly pressed military uniform that held many medals and stripes which hung neatly across his jacket. His shoes shined with perfection that morning as he walked slowly and proudly through the home that Christmas day.

The smile on George's face began to grow brighter, lightening his face with each step. He strolled across the floor in each room, giving his approval to Joyce's selection of the home. He looked even more dignified in person. The picture of him that remained plastered on the living room wall didn't compare to his physical presence.

In his hands, he held an armful of packages in which all the children saw. No one questioned him regarding the packages, as they all were too engrossed in admiring his attire. George continued to enter each room. After he had completed his walk through of the house, he returned into the living room where he finally spoke.

"How have my babies been doing?"

The children all ran up to him giving him hugs and kisses. He began handing out gifts. Kim too followed to receive the gifts that he graciously gave out to each child. She stood in line waiting somewhat impatiently behind her older siblings for the line to grow shorter. As she approached her father, who stood straight and stern, he appear somewhat a giant to her. Her heart dropped in disappointment as she clearly saw that his hands were now empty. The gifts he once held were all gone. Tears of sorrow and disappointment rolled uncontrollably down her petite face as she stood in grief. No words could express the misery she felt.

George ran out of the house while Joyce consoled Kim who

stood in distraught. She was crying frantically as she watched her brothers and sisters opening and playing with their new toys.

"What is wrong sweetie? Please don't cry. You didn't think that I was going to forget my baby girl, did you," George said as he returned into the house? He displayed a proud look upon his face.

Kim's eyes brightened as she hopped out of her mother's arms and went running back towards George. He handed her the biggest doll baby she had ever seen. Her tears now melted away as she displayed a cheerful smile upon her face. She now appeared as joyous as her siblings.

The doll stood up as tall as Kim. It wore a beautiful white evening dress with white silk bows around her curly ponytails and silk shoes to match her attire. After giving George a big hug, she grabbed the doll out of his hand and joined her siblings in the living room where they all played with their new gifts. The Tucker's home rang out with laughter and cheers that Christmas. It was truly the happiest occasion they had felt in years.

"Whose car is that parked in the driveway?" Joyce asked her husband, hours later. The tone in her voice revealed her obvious irritation.

Joyce had begun drinking early that morning, even before breakfast. It was apparent that she was preparing herself for George's arrival.

"That's your Christmas present," George explained.

"If it is my Christmas present, then why have you been driving it all over town? Where are my keys? Go ahead and just be honest... you know that it is your car. How dare you come home with a new car when your children and I have been here for the past three years starving!" Joyce yelled frantically.

"Calm down mama, let's go see the car," Bobby insisted, aware of her drunken pattern. He and the other children ran to the back door. A beautiful white shiny Cadillac was parked in the driveway. The children smiled brightly. Immediately, the Tucker children pleaded to go for a ride in the new car.

"You children might as well come on and get back in this house... right now! Your father is going to take that car right back where he bought it!" Joyce said with determination. She yelled at them through the screen door.

The children ignored her command as Bobby led the way to the Cadillac.

"Why do you always have to ruin everything Joyce?" George asked. "You children go ahead, listen to your mother and get back into the house. I'm going over to my mother's," George said as he getting into his car. He drove away rapidly.

To Joyce's dismay, he failed to return home that evening. She had waited up most of the night for his return. She got the children dressed early that morning and drove over to Grandma Dina's house to see if he was there. Of course, not before she had taken a couple of sips from her flask before leaving the

16

house. She had to prepare herself for what she was about to encounter. The new car was parked in front of Grandma Dina's house, when they arrived. Joyce knocked violently on the front door.

"Hello Joyce, what are you doing here this early in the morning with all of the kids?" Grandma Dina asked.

"Is George here?"

"Yes, he's still asleep," Grandma Dina expressed to Joyce.

Joyce stormed forcefully passed her and went into the bedroom to wake George.

"You two have better go outside with this mess!" Grandma Dina yelled.

Joyce stormed pass her into the bedroom where George slept. He arose quickly as she entered the room and moved rapidly in a rampage, rushing out of the bedroom onto the front porch. Joyce followed him out of the door and onto the porch.

They commenced into an intense argument.

"You need to explain to me just why you would go out and buy that car without consulting with me! You should have checked with me to see if there was something else more irrelevant that we needed here at home. You drive up here with that big fancy car... which is bigger than our home!"

"Why can't I ever do anything to please you Joyce? You don't appreciate anything. Everything is just an argument with you! You needed a new car, Joyce! Look at that old piece of crap you've been driving! It's standing on one leg," George expressed.

"You don't know what we need because you haven't been around to see what it is we need!"

The children continued to watch and listen to their parents' heated conversation. The discussion, which mainly centered on the new car and the fact that George had not been coming home to visit, appeared to persist for hours.

After their voices settled, Joyce put the children into her old worn out 1957 station wagon and drove them back to the house. George didn't come back to his mother's that evening however he came to his wife's home to say his farewells. He was to return to Texas that afternoon.

After his return to Texas, George withdrew from sending

child support monies home for the children. Joyce was mortified; she cried nearly every night. She also began to fall deeper and deeper into the bottle. With each tear she shed, she indulged in another drink. The year became even more strenuous with her unsuccessful attempts to contact him. The family continued to suffer, as Joyce was full of pride. She didn't want a soul in Rocking Barrel to know the fact that her husband had ran off, refusing to take care of his children. Joyce hid his apparent abandonment from her family, the neighbors and from military officials. In her heart she was hopeful that he would eventually come back and honor his wedding vows.

Purchasing a sewing machine, Joyce began to sew the children's clothes in an effort to conceal the fact that she had no money to buy them any. This brought some excitement back into her life as she minimally stayed off the bottle long enough to complete her projects.

She signed up at the elementary school to do some substitute teaching. Many afternoons when she returned home from work, she was stressed.

"I wish that Victor were here... he would definitely keep you children in line," she would say so often.

Victor, the eldest son, left home immediately after graduating from high school, June of 1965. He moved to New Jersey and didn't return home for a period of two years. Although no one knew exactly what it was that he was doing, or why he had chosen to go there. Joyce often worried about his state of being and stated so when she was drunk.

She went on several assignments at the school but eventually had to give this up too. She remained at home with the young children because the older children had become stubborn and disobedient. They were no longer reliable. She could no longer depend on them coming straight home from school to look over the younger children.

In November of 1967, the Tucker's home sounded out with joy of enthusiasm and high spirits because Victor called to say that he would be coming home to visit. Joyce screamed out with shouts of exalted praises and glory, pealing throughout the house.

She was quite delighted that Victor had chosen to come home for Thanksgiving.

When Victor arrived home, he was awed and astonished at the fact that there was no turkey or ham on the table. He couldn't remember a holiday season that the Tucker's home didn't smell of turkey roasting and ham baking. The scent remained absent, sparking his curiosity. He was even more concerned when he saw Mr. Conrad, an old neighbor, in their backyard. Mr. Conrad was wringing a chicken's neck. His demeanor, as he stumbled, showed him to be as intoxicated as Joyce. Victor was surely certain that the chicken was for his mother to clean and prepare for the Thanksgiving feast. Along with the chicken lay a skinned squirrel with its hind legs pointing upward in the air, apparently waiting to be cooked.

"Where is the turkey and ham, mother? I know daddy sent you money to buy the children a decent meal. Why are these black birds laid out on the counter? I certainly hope that you do not plan on cooking and serving them as well," he said.

"No, those are for me," Joyce said. "You know they are a delicacy and no, your daddy has not sent money home. He hasn't sent money home in almost a year."

"Why not? Why haven't you reported him to his superiors?

He has to send money home. The military has strict laws against men who do not support their children. I'll drive you down to the Veterans Administration before I return home."

Victor stayed in town long enough to assist Joyce with her personal affairs. She filled all the paper work out that she was given and returned them promptly. She was surprised and quite content with the positive responses she received. Even more so with the provisions she received from the Veterans Administration. She received an emergency check that very day. Not long thereafter, she began to receive her child support money in the mail from George. Before Christmas, everything was back to normal and the children had the best Christmas that year thanks to the Veterans Administration and Social Services.

Chapter 5

After serving twenty-six years in the United States Army, George finally retired and returned home to be with his family in early January of 1968. The Tucker house during the first several months of his return appeared pleasant; there was a true family environment now that George was home. An immediate calm came about Joyce, which shifted the children's chaotic behavior into an abrupt peace.

Regrettably, George's strong desire to put his military tactics to practice brought about a disruption in the home. His militant attitude advantageously showed its face as he appointed the girls to wash dishes, sweep the floors and dress the bedding each day. He equally chastised the boys, appointing them to take out the trash and uphold their bathroom duties. On the weekends, all the children and Joyce participated in cleaning windows, cupboards and baseboards. The family time Joyce wished for never became a reality.

Although the younger children welcomed and appreciated the new order that George brought into the home, the older boys often rebelled against his stern rules. Often defiant, the boys were punished with having to complete fifty or more push-ups when they rebelled or refused to complete their chores.

Sassy and Rosetta shared the "Dorm Room," an isolated bedroom located in the rear of the Tucker's home — the "Dorm". Obtaining the Dorm was a tradition in the Tucker's home. This meant that when entering your senior year of high school that you gained the gratification of acquiring the Dorm. The Dorm was used as a means of preparing the Tucker children for the real world. It was the closest thing to a college atmosphere, since there was no way that George could afford to send twelve children off to college.

Victor, however, chose not to occupy the Dorm his senior year. Instead, he chose to sleep out in the den on the sofa bed. Rosetta decided once Victor moved to New Jersey that she would move into the den. Rosetta's willingness to take over the sofa bed in the den gave Sassy, who was not yet a senior, seniority to acquire the Dorm.

George was adamant in enforcing his strong conviction that his daughters leave his home after graduating from high school. His demands were so notoriously known and repetitively done that even Kim was cognizant to the fact that she too must leave home after graduating. The boys always had the option to stay or leave but the girls were immediately forced into the real world.

"Women always seem to find a man to take care of them in this world," George so often told Joyce. "A man is surely not going to find a woman who is willing to take care of him," his excuse of allowing the men to remain in the home.

As for his daughters — Rosetta, after graduating from high school, married Ray who had received a full scholarship to attend one of the universities to get his law degree in Washington, DC. She worked as an administrative assistant at the same university. Rosetta smoothed the way for the Tucker girl's direction in departing Rocking Barrel.

Sassy, only a year younger than Rosetta was the next Tucker girl to leave home. However, under strenuous circumstances and not voluntarily, she got pregnant during her senior year of high school. She did a terrific job of concealing it from her parents, however, before summer's end, her secret had been revealed within her ninth month. The house was in a terrible uproar that afternoon Joyce learned of Sassy's pregnancy.

"What in the world is going on in here?"

"Didn't I tell you guys to clean up this mess?" Sassy said now entering the room.

"Sassy don't you come in here, a day late, telling them to

25

clean the house. I asked you to ensure that it be clean by the time I got home from work. So, why is it in shambles?" Joyce asked.

She stood looking angrily at Sassy and with her hands upon her hips awaiting an answer.

"These are your children and I do not have time to watch them every second of the day," Sassy said.

"What, what did you say to me... you must have lost your mind Sassy!"

"Never mind," Sassy replied turning her back to Joyce. She began to walk away.

"Don't you dare turn your back on me when I am talking to you!" Joyce yelled. She grabbed Sassy forcefully by her blouse and so tightly, ripping it from her back.

Sassy turned to retrieve her blouse from which now lay on the floor. Her stomach was swollen and with stretch marks that undeniably revealed her secret... her pregnancy now confirmed. This alleviated any disbelief in which Joyce may have had. Her eyes too fill up with tears of disappointment. The room for a moment quiets with stillness as everyone absorbed the truth.

"Not only are you blatantly trifling and obviously lazy and now you have laid yourself down and gotten knocked up as well,"

Joyce cried. "Who is the father of this child you're carrying, or do you even know?" Sassy gave no answer. She ran into the restroom and locked the door.

"Come out of there," Joyce insisted, banging loudly on the door. "You're going to have to come out of there sooner or later! Clean up this mess!" Joyce demanded. She spoke directly to the younger children who sat and stood around watching in disbelief.

With devastation and hurt in her heart, Joyce retreated into her bedroom where she remained until later that afternoon when George returned home from work. Sassy inched her way out of the restroom and went into her bedroom. She remained there until she was awakened by George and Joyce's uproar in the house.

"She can get the hell out of here because I'm not running a whorehouse for unwed mothers! I'm not going to allow a house full of prostitutes to lie up in my house having illegitimate babies! Sassy, you get the hell out of my damn house! I want you gone today!"

Sassy ran hysterically down the street to her girlfriend's house as desperation poured within her young heart. She reluctantly explained her heartbreaking situation to her friend, Marietta. She sequentially sought guidance from her mother, Mrs.

Victoria. Although quite sympathetic to Sassy's situation, Mrs. Victoria informed her with tact and certainty that there was no way that she could allow her to live in her home.

"I'm sorry to hear of your troubles child but you know that I can't allow you to stay here. Especially with your family feeling the way they do about your situation."

"I understand Mrs. Victoria and I'm sorry to be a bother this time of the night. May I please use your telephone to call my sister Rosetta in Washington, DC?"

"Sure you can."

Sassy made her telephone call as she frantically explained her situation to Rosetta. She told her all about how George had put her out. Rosetta insisted that she come there immediately, to live with her and Ray. They wired Sassy money to catch the bus. Sassy was packed and on the bus headed for Washington, DC the following day.

Rosetta and Ray picked Sassy up from the bus station where she sat waiting patiently. Sassy looked at Rosetta and realized that she too was with child.

"I'm so sorry to be such a bother to you and Ray," Sassy said. You should have told me that you were pregnant too. I wouldn't have come had I known."

"No, well where else might you have gone?" Rosetta said cynically while embracing her sister tightly.

In less than two weeks after arriving to Washington, Sassy gave birth to her son, Jasper. Two months following his birth Rosetta gave birth to her son, Little Ray. Sassy found blessings in Washington as she landed herself an administrative assistant position. She continued to live with Rosetta and Ray for a couple of months. She saved enough money to get her and Jasper their place.

Bobby, the senior in the house now, inherited the Dorm. He was so enthusiastic about acquiring the room that it took him less than an hour to move all of his belongings. The fact that he would not have to share a bed with any one overwhelmed him. He praised the privacy; however, it wasn't long that he realized that being adjacent to the one and only restroom in the Tucker's home was surely — no blessing.

"More of a curse," Bobby often said.

Bobby was the worst at not following George's rules. He would constantly try to control the younger children by mimicking his father's conduct. He would force his younger brothers and sisters to iron his clothes and to do his household chores. If anyone refused to follow his orders, Bobby would beat them.

In the middle bedroom, the other Tucker children slept on their bunk beds. Joyce and Kim shared the top-bunk while Ginger and Mona slept on the bottom bunk. Borne and Nicholas slept on the top bunk. Felicia, the oldest sister living at home, enjoyed the pleasure of the bottom bunk to herself, while waiting patiently to occupy the Dorm.

Often on Sundays after finishing their supper, George and Joyce would pile the children into the car and drive over to visit Grandma Sara. Calvin, now seventeen years of age, continued to live with Grandma Sara. One afternoon when the family visited Grandma Sara's home, Kim walked in excitedly. She immediately acknowledged Calvin's presence, since it was such a rare occasion for the Tuckers to find him at home and not hanging out with his friends.

"Hi Uncle Calvin," Kim said, delighted to see his face.

"Honey, Calvin is not your uncle, he's your brother," Joyce said.

"She is so stupid!" Nicholas insisted.

"Well I didn't know. Why does he live here with Grandma Sara and not with us?"

"Oh go sit down," Joyce said. Calvin's name was only spoken occasionally in the Tucker's home. The conversations, as Kim entered the room, coming to an abrupt halt. The rumor around Rocking Barrel was that Calvin was not truly a Tucker child and that Joyce had gotten pregnant with him in 1950. During this time George was away fighting in the Korean War.

Whispers and laughter rung out as everyone began to laugh hysterically at the fact that Kim thought that Calvin was her uncle. Kim was not pleased that she was being ridiculed and Calvin too didn't find the situation humorous. She and Calvin both found it rather frustrating; the fact that Kim didn't know that he was her brother.

"Don't worry Kim... I'll be your uncle if that's who you want me to be," he chuckled.

With his words of comfort, she now began to smile and as the family settled down. They all began to talk amongst one another forgetting the incident.

Calvin continued to live with Grandma Sara until he too finally moved to Washington, DC. He decided to make it on his own with little contact with his siblings, Victor, Rosetta, or Sassy.

Bobby and Felicia fought constantly, because Felicia persistently refused to follow his commands. One afternoon he ordered her to go into the kitchen to prepare spaghetti for supper. Joyce had been drinking increasingly all morning long. She had passed out in her bedroom in a drunken snooper, before feeding the children.

Felicia refused his demand, as usual. Bobby went into the kitchen and began boiling the water as if for the spaghetti noodles. He and Felicia continued to argue screaming from room to room, with Bobby in the kitchen and Felicia in her bedroom. Moments later, in a heated rage, Bobby ran into the bedroom and poured the scorching water on Felicia's leg.

Joyce awakened immediately after hearing Felicia's screams of agony. She rushed into the room and grabbed her up, rushing her to the emergency room. The doctors said that Felicia sustained second-degree burns. For Bobby's protection Joyce told the police that Felicia had accidentally dropped the water.

George was furious with her when she told him the news of what Bobby had done to Felicia.

"Why would you take up for him? He should be punished! I know what I'm going to do," he said.

George called the local reform school immediately. "Pack your things boy! You're getting out of my house!" he said.

Bobby packed his clothes in silence. The rest of the family sat quietly and saddened at the outcome. An hour later, officers arrived to the home to take Bobby to the boy's home. Bobby never shed a tear as they led him out the door.

"George, I believe that we could have handled the situation better by shouldering the burden instead of sending him away. Show a little more sensitivity and patience with the children, instead of trying to program them. You come home implementing these strict and cumbersome convictions. That is unnecessary. We had no problem while you were away and not on one occasion did I feel that I had to send one of my children away from home!" she scolded.

"He could have killed Felicia or perhaps one of the other children. I will not accept this kind of behavior in my home."

As the months passed by, George constantly threatened the children that they too would be sent away if they rebelled against him. This escalated deep scars of resentment towards their father.

Felicia moved into the Dorm, in her junior year of high school, while Bobby was away. Ginger moved down to the bottom bunk, to sleep alone. Ginger and Felicia were both happy about finally having their own bed. Although a bit distraught, when Bobby returned home that following year and reassigned to the Dorm. Felicia, however, refused to let this spoil her senior year. With no quarrel, she moved back into the middle room where she slept on the bottom bunk with Ginger.

Felicia excelled tremendously in school her senior year. She obtained academic honors in many areas and flourishing substantially in her personal life. She became a different individual... no longer shying away but popular. She had become out going and to some extent a different soul. Felicia was honored with being crowned prom queen and Miss Rocking Barrel in the city beauty pageant. After graduating from high school, she participated in the state competition where she became runner-up. She sung, Roberta Flack's "Killing Me Softly" in each pageant. Her voice tone was somewhat more that of Minnie Rippertons's winning over the judges' hearts. Disappointed in not having won the state competition she decided that she also; like her older sisters, would move to Washington, DC.

Bobby married his high school sweetheart, Barbara, after

graduating and they moved to New Jersey to live. Mona and Ginger both graduated the next following two-years and moved to Washington. Little-Joyce was the next to graduate, she and Borne — the twins. Unfortunately, when the time came, Borne didn't graduate because he had apparently missed too many days by playing hooky.

Joyce, after graduating decided to go to New Jersey to live with Victor. He promised to get her a job in the banking industry and he proved true to his word. As Nicholas too graduated, he and Borne chose to stay around Rocking Barrel.

Rosetta was the key source, which opened the door to the big city for the Tucker women. Kim too hoped to someday make Washington, DC her home as her five sisters before her had done. Time passed and exceedingly quicker than she had expected. Astonishingly so the time was at hand that she too was graduating and leaving Rocking Barrel.

Maverick, Kim's old and dear friend, promised her that he would come to take her out of town. He offered to ride her to Washington, DC

Chapter 6

Impetuously Kim stood in her front yard anxiously awaiting his arrival. She was quite excited to be leaving that despicable town — Rocking Barrel. Kim genuinely felt confined and drawn to its barriers. She so longed to discover a way out of its hold, which grasped her tightly.

The harsh winter wind blew roughly against her face even with the bright wintry sun beaming forcefully through the clouds. The sunshine bounced indelibly against the gold sparkles of her tweed coat. This sparked a large glimpse of gold that shined radiantly on the street in front of her that appears to taunt her to stay.

"Where is Maverick?" she wondered. It had been more than two hours since he telephoned.

"I'll be there shortly," he said.

Maverick lived only fifteen minutes away from where she now stood. Surely, he had not given second thoughts and changed his mind about riding her to Washington.

"What could be keeping him from fulfilling his promise to her? He knows how desperately I want to get away from here. He was one person in whom she could trust and depend upon in Rocking Barrel. He'll show... I know he will. How can I possibly be standing here having these negative thoughts regarding him? He has to come," she thought.

His presence would surely grant her the strength she needed to demolish the curse she sensed upon her spirit. As the hand of time passed quickly, she indulged in recollections of forgotten time. She stood reminiscing about all the awful times there in Rocking Barrel. She reminisced also about the enjoyable times that she had encountered as well. Remarkably revealing... the dreadful memories rekindled in her mind. She tried desperately to block them away.

She began to think about Jessica — her closest childhood friend. Jessica was the only person with whom she shared her deepest secrets: her emotions, in-depth feelings, her first love and her worst nightmares. She loved Jessica dearly and as a sister. They had been friends since she was five years old

Jessica had beautiful brown eyes and silky brown hair, which flowed down her back and onto her shoulders like water flowing down a waterfall. Her skin was silky and smooth. Kim and

Jessica was the envy of many other young girls in town. As they grew, they became the desire of many young boys and quite a few older men in Rocking Barrel. Kim was just as pretty with her shiny sandy brown hair, matching her sandy caramel complexion. Unlike Jessica — she was very insecure about her beauty.

The summer was the best time of year for the girls, because there was so much to do, unlike any other months. Rocking Barrel, known for its beautiful trees, which blossomed all year round. A typical summer day for the girls was to go to the park and play tennis, cards, or other sporting activities. Mostly they just liked walking and enjoying each other's company. The girls were inseparable friends. Therefore when Jessica's mother, Mrs. Barber, decided unconditionally that she would leave her husband — the girls were devastated.

Kim couldn't imagine being apart from her and them being apart from one another. She was envious of Jessica for getting an opportunity to leave Rocking Barrel. Not all who were born and bred in Rocking Barrel gain this opportunity. Jessica was going to escape its solidly forceful barriers. She felt that maybe it would be better for Jessica if she were to leave town. Jessica had gotten out of control. Especially, since she had acquired such a flirtatious behavior about her over the summer. Her appetite for men had gone beyond the young boys, as she grew utterly fonder and more seductive towards many of the married men in town.

"I've had enough of you and your drunken ways," Kim overheard Mrs. Barber say one night when she slept over at Jessica's home.

The frustration they bestowed on one another that evening was horrendous, as they hit one another relentlessly. Standing in a corner the girls watched fearfully as Mrs. Barber pushed Mr. Barber to the floor with his head hitting the corner of the oak wood nightstand. To the girls' dismay, Jessica's parents indulged in a horrible fistfight. Certainly, this incident confirmed the Barber's break-up.

"I want a divorce and I mean it this time!" Mrs. Barber yelled to him as he lay in defeat. She turned and walked out of the front door. Mr. Barber was unable to give her any response.

Kim arrived home that next morning to find that her home too was in turmoil. She entered the front door and observed broken pieces of glass on the floor. As she advanced into the kitchen, she noticed that there were broken plates on the clear tile. She didn't ask any questions, however she picked up the broom and began to clean up the area. She went into her bedroom and joined her brothers and sisters in their silence.

Later that afternoon, Jessica showed up at her door with her eyes full of tears.

"Hi Jessica... come in," Kim insisted. Jessica stood at the door with her eyes puffy and swollen.

"My mother has still not returned home and we are concerned about her. She has never left the house without at least calling to inform us of her whereabouts."

"In all likelihood Jessica, she is probably sitting right at home this very instant."

Smiling in agreement, Jessica nodded and said, "You're probably right."

"Come on, I'll go with you to see if she's returned."

They went back to Jessica's house but unfortunately, her mom was not there. Jessica's eyes began to tear up again and the telephone began to ring. Jessica and Kim anxiously eased their way to the edge of the door to listen as Mr. Barber lifted up the receiver. They listened meticulously to every detail of his conversation to find out if it was Mrs. Barber on the other end.

"Where are you? When are you coming home? Well if your decision has been made and your mind is made up, then I suggest that you go right ahead. I surely can't stop you or change your mind," Mr. Barber said.

His voice revealed his disappointment and he Forcefully slammed down the telephone.

Kim and Jessica ran abruptly into the kitchen where they sat at the table trying not to be obvious of their ease dropping. Jessica gazed at Kim as Mr. Barber entered the room. They were glad that her mother was safe.

"I'll see you later," Jessica uttered.

Kim asked no questions as she quickly advanced towards the door. She knew that it would be best if she didn't return to Jessica's home for a while but wait for Jessica to come to visit her when she was calm. Kim waited patiently for three days, when Jessica showed up knocking at her door.

"Hi Kim," she whispered softly.

"What's wrong?"

Kim put her arms around Jessica and led her into the house. She stood there with those same somber teardrops.

"It is true, my mother is going to leave my daddy. She's going to be taking me along with her. The rest of my sisters and brothers will remain here with my father," she cried hysterically.

"Where are you going? When will you be leaving?" Kim asked.

"Today. We are supposed to leave out today," she told. "I can't believe that she is doing this to me. Well I just wanted to come by to say goodbye."

She gave Kim a big hug as the news came as a shock to her. She tried desperately to hide her devastation from Jessica who was already quite distraught.

"Don't worry Jessica, I am certain that it will be okay. I'm sure that you will do well in Washington," she said trying to console her friend's fears.

"What will I do without you, Jessie?"

"What do I know about living in Washington, DC? Besides, I have never even been outside of the city limits of Rocking Barrel. This is certainly going to ruin my life!" she cried out as she continued to express her strong feelings of disappointment.

"Look how well my sisters have done there in Washington," Kim said.

She tried to remain cool for Jessica's sake, as well as her own sake. She didn't want Jessica to leave Rocking Barrel but there was nothing to be done to rectify her parent's relationship.

"She's only taking you?"

Kim pondered a reason as to why Jessica was the only Barber child to be leaving town with her mother.

"Just me? It's not fair that everyone else gets to stay here in Rocking Barrel. "Why do I have to be the one to be separated from the rest of my family? I haven't done anything wrong to deserve this cruelty! Why am I being punished because they have decided to get a divorce?"

An hour later after walking Jessica back to her house, Kim found that Mrs. Barber had finished packing the car. She was waiting impatiently for Jessica's return so they could be on their way to Washington. Unfortunately, the time had come that she would loose her best friend. They were on their way, as Kim stood with Jessica's family as the car pulled out of the driveway.

After Jessica left Kim's life changed. She had climbed into her own little shell because she now had no friends. She would come straight home from school. Once there she would go into her room and start her homework. Her grades improved tremendously.

Enduring three months of boredom, she realized that she could no longer continue to alienate herself. Kim considered ways to occupy her time and after overhearing a couple of girls on the school bus talking about a neighborhood church choir, she decided to join the group. Immersed with participating in the church choir, Kim found a newly developed inner-peace. She felt a calm within her heart and spirit, which changed her life.

She acquired morals and stability as she obtained an inner self-confidence that was beneficial to her throughout her life encounters. In particular, Kim became fond of the Bible verse 1 John 4:4: "Ye are of God, little children and have overcome them: because greater is he that is in you, than he that is in the world."

This Bible verse helped her through many trials and tribulations as she grew in life. Kim dedicated her life to Christ that school year.

"Come on Kim, you can go with us," Nicholas yelled from up the street.

She found it hard to believe that he agreed to let her come along with him and Borne. When they arrived at the park, Kim couldn't help but notice someone sitting alone on one of the benches. This girl sat with her elbows placed downward on the table and her hands resting up on her cheeks. For a moment, Kim thought that it was Jessica. She walked faster to meet her long lost friend. As she got closer to the girl, she realized that she was not Jessica. However, she continued to look a lot like her. Kim wanted her to be Jessica.

"Hi how are you?" the girl said as Kim approached the bench.

"Just fine," Kim smiled. She was glad to see a friendly face.

"I'm Leslie."

"Hello, Leslie. I thought you were someone else sitting there."

"I just moved down the street. We were bored, so we decided to come to the park."

"Who else is with you?"

Kim looked around to see why Leslie sat there alone.

"Danny, my brother and I came together."

She pointed to Danny who was on the basketball court with nine other guys including Borne and Nicholas.

"My brothers Borne and Nicholas are out there playing too. That's Borne in the green shirt. Nicholas is the short one wearing the blue shirt," Kim pointed out to her.

As they sat on the bench, the conversation came easy for both Kim and Leslie as they realized they had a lot in common. It was almost as if she were talking to Jessica the way in which she and Leslie understood one another.

"Come on walk with me and I'll show you where I live. Maybe you can stop by sometimes, instead of coming to the park

45

to sit by yourself," Kim said. "My house is right down the street."

"So is my house," Leslie told.

They stopped in to Kim's house first where she introduced Leslie to her mother and sisters. They then were off to Leslie's house.

Once they arrived to Leslie's house Kim met her mother, Ms. Smiley and her sister, Maggie. Kim found Maggie to be very intriguing. She was the first deaf person she had ever encountered. It was amazing to her to watch Maggie and Leslie sign. Maggie showed off such elegance with each word, as she spoke with her hands.

"Do you think you can teach me to sign? Kim asked of Leslie. I would love to learn to speak to Maggie the way that you do Leslie. Watching the two of you speak was wonderful. Something I have never seen before."

"Sure, I'll teach you" Leslie replied.

"I'm surprised that you are willing to learn the language."

With Maggie away at school for the week, Kim welcomed this time to impress her by learning to sign. Kim went over to Leslie's house every evening to learn how to sign. When Maggie returned home, she was highly impressed that she had taken the time out to learn her language. Her face lit up with astonishment and delight, as Kim could see that she appreciated her initiative.

Chapter 7

Jessica returned home shortly before the summer ended. Mrs. Barber sent her back home, because she was getting into a lot of trouble in Washington. She was also doing badly in school. Kim was delighted at the news when Tammy, Jessica's sister, informed her that she would be returning home.

Jessica came immediately to Kim's house, after settling down. They rushed off to the park and sat on their favorite bench. The two talked for hours about Jessica's experience in the big city. Although Kim had been to Washington, DC to visit her sisters during the summer, she still thought it was exciting that Jessica had actually lived there an entire year.

"So, how was it Jessica?"

"How was what?"

"How was life in the big city? What else would I be talking about?"

"I wasn't thrilled with living in the city. I guess I'm a country girl at heart. I missed you and my family and just wanted to come home. The girls there weren't fond of me and I was always fighting and getting suspensions from school. Every other week I was getting into trouble. The girls there were so much more mature than the girls in Rocking Barrel," Joyce concluded.

Jessica's words were very shocking to Kim. The fact that she would admit the city girls to be more mature, as Kim recalled how Jessica held such maturity about her before going to the city.

"Well I'm glad you've returned Jessica, I really missed you," she said while embracing her with a hug.

From that day the girls were reunited once again, spending the entire summer together. After the summer ended, Jessica began to act different, changing drastically. She acted as if she were too good to associate with Kim. She appeared to have only men on her mind. She was more interested in spending time with the men in town and riding around in their fancy cars.

Kim had gone over to Jessica's house to get her to go to the park, as they had done so often before.

"Do you want to go to the park?" she asked.

"No I don't want to go to the park. Why do you keep asking me that every time that you come over? I'm not interested in spending my precious time playing in the park, like some child."

"Well... what do you want to do then?" Kim asked.

"I'm getting too old for that kind of stuff, Kim. Here comes my ride... I'll have to get back with you maybe later on today."

Jessica walked away from Kim, walking off towards a navy-blue Cadillac that had pulled up in front of her house. She got into the car.

"Good-bye Kim." "Good-bye Jessica," Kim said, looking dumbfounded. She walked away and headed over to Leslie's home to see if maybe she had time to spend with her. It was apparently obvious to Kim that Jessica had other plans that of course didn't include her.

"Hi Leslie, what are you doing... are you busy?"

"No, come on in. What's wrong with you?"

"Nothing."

"You look like you have a lot on your mind."

"Well now that you ask, I'm kind of worried about my friend, Jessica. Do you remember me telling you that she has moved back to town after living in Washington, DC for a year?"

"Yes, I remember you telling me about her."

"Do you think you can go over to her house with me a little later to meet her? She's not home now," she explained.

"Sure, I'll go meet her. Why are you so worried? "

"She hasn't been herself since she returned home."

Leslie and Kim walked over to Kim's house where they sat around the house listening to records and talking to Kim's sisters.

Leslie helped Kim and her sisters clean the house before it was time for Joyce to return home from work.

Joyce had taken on a job as a cook at a local restaurant. She did this primarily to get out of the house and away from the children. In addition, she wanted spending money for herself and the children.

Kim expected that by Jessica meeting Leslie that she would reconsider spending time with the men that she was seeing. Kim felt that Leslie and Jessica would definitely be able to relate to one other, since they were the same age. She hoped that Leslie would be a good influence and that she could deal with Jessica on a different level than she could. Kim thought that Jessica would show interest in hanging with the two them.

They returned to Jessica's house and she introduced the two. Jessica and Leslie hit it off wonderfully. The three of them spent that day together and many more. Jessica seemed to be content whenever Leslie was around, appearing to forget all about the men in whom she had let control her life.

The next summer was great now that the three were constantly together. However, the summer soon passed and Jessica was a free spirit, once again. Not even Leslie could hold her attention once the summer passed.

Bored with the repetitive activities, she lingered out seeking more adventure, thus returning to her past lifestyle. She began to push away from Kim and Leslie. She began to date the older men again.

One afternoon, when they went to get her, Jessica told Kim that she couldn't leave the house because she was on punishment. Kim knew that this had to be just an excuse, because in all the years that she had known Jessica, Mr. Barber had never punished her. He had never refused to let her out with Kim.

Borne, the green-eyed bandit fell in love with Leslie the first day he met her in the park. He soon won her over. It was shocking for Kim to believe that the two were dating. They were quite an item a little before the summer ended. As time drifted on in there relationship, Borne became very possessive of Leslie. He refused to let her spend time with anyone other than himself.

With Jessica not coming around as much, Leslie also began to break away from Kim. She considered Kim too young for her now that Jessica was no longer with them.

Ironically Leslie tried to hang out with Kim's sisters Joyce, Ginger and Mona. They however considered Leslie quite too young to hang out with them. It wasn't long before Leslie and Kim

51

were spending little to no time together. She welcomed the weekends when Maggie would come home from school and in the summer. They would go swimming, playing basketball or tennis... since Leslie was no longer available.

Ms. Smiley hated the fact that Leslie, Kim and Jessica Were no longer spending time together. She was concern that Leslie had begun to spend too much time with Borne. She hated the fact that Leslie had such strong feelings for him at such a young age and wanted to keep the two apart. Even though she had forbidden Leslie from seeing him this couldn't keep them apart. It wasn't until Borne began to spend time elsewhere that she became content. Although one telephone call from Leslie informing him of her renowned interest sent him back into her arms.

He wanted Leslie so much and wanted her undivided attention. He had gotten involved with someone else, but broke up with her once he received Leslie's call. Leslie often bragged about this when she could find an ear that was willing to listen.

Borne began to go over to her house frequently because Ms. Smiley was working third shift. He and Leslie found this time to be quite pleasurable. They took full advantage of their time alone and they continued to do so all year. At least they did until time finally caught up with them.

"Come on in here Leslie!" Ms. Smiley demanded.

She yelled at her furiously. Pulling her by the arm, she dragged her violently into the Tucker's home. Her intentions were to come over that afternoon primarily to inform George and Joyce of Leslie's pregnancy.

"How could you have been so reckless?"

She slapped Leslie relentlessly on the backside of her head that Leslie screamed from the anguish.

"What is going on out here?" Joyce exclaimed, rushing out into the kitchen. "Why are you snatching and beating on this child like this?"

Leslie continued her cries of pain.

"She's gone and gotten herself knocked-up after being seduced by your son!" Ms. Smiley screamed.

"Lower your voice and have a seat. Let's discuss this sensibly; it isn't everyone's personal business. You're certainly not helping the situation by beating her. Everyone in the neighborhood is watching," Joyce insisted.

"You're utterly correct... and I apologize," she said. I am just so disappointed in Leslie. I feel so betrayed. How could they

53

possibly have been so irresponsible? I've asked Leslie numerous times if she and Borne were sexually involved and she continuously denied the truth. I even discussed the issue of getting her on birth control pills in the event that they may consider having sex. Leslie assured me that she remained a virgin and sex was far from their mind. I refuse to let her stay in my house! I can barely take care of the three children that I have now. I don't know how she thinks that we are going to take care of this one! In all honesty, I'll have you know that Leslie has some brainless delusion of actually keeping this child. I absolutely forbid it!"

Leslie got up, went into Kim's room and laid down on one of the empty beds. She began to cry. Kim sat at the edge of the bed, next to her. She watched her quietly and with pity. She looked deep inside herself for words of encouragement but she could find none.

Minutes later George arrived home to find Ms. Smiley and Joyce engrossed in an intense argument.

"What is going on in here? I could hear you as I got out of the car!

"Perhaps you and I should discuss this matter. Your wife just doesn't seem to comprehend or receive the seriousness of this matter," Ms. Smiley informed George.

"Excuse me!" Joyce interrupted.

"What is going on Joyce?" George asked.

"Leslie's pregnant."

"Yes, my child's pregnant by your son and I'd like to know just what do you intend to do about this matter. Your son has ruined her life," Ms. Smiley said.

"What else can be done regarding her predicament except for her to have the child? George said.

"She can't have this baby!" Ms. Smiley uttered.

"They are much too young to get married but he will have to marry her. She can't take care of this child alone," George insisted.

"That's unthinkable! I already called the clinic about the possibility of her having an abortion," Ms. Smiley informed. "I didn't have the three hundred dollars for the abortion. If I did, then I certainly would have taken her there before confronting you with this issue."

"That is murder! I don't want anything to do with the killing of this baby," Joyce said.

"I sincerely hope that you are prepared to let Leslie and the baby come here to live with you because they definitely will not be welcomed in my house," Ms. Smiley confirmed.

"Go get my check book Joyce. I'll pay for the abortion."

Joyce left the room to retrieve George's checkbook.

"I'm really sorry about the whole thing," Ms. Smiley said. George sat impatiently awaiting Joyce's return.

"I'll call to make the appointment in the morning."

He immediately began to write out the check.

"I'll just write it out to you Ms. Smiley."

"Come on Leslie. Let's go!" Ms. Smiley yelled as she grabbed the check from George's hand. "I'll call you to let you know how everything went."

Leslie and her mother left the home abruptly.

Weeks went by and neither George nor Joyce heard any word of confirmation from Ms. Smiley concerning the abortion. Kim relayed to her parents and Borne, Ms. Smile's words of warning that Borne stay away from her home and her daughter.

Confined to the house for a month, Borne became bored and started going back to the park to play basketball. Leslie, however, remained on punishment for several months following her pregnancy. She was band from the park as well as unable to leave her house after school.

When the time approached for Leslie to return to a normal life she ensured her mother that she would stay as far away from Borne as possible. She did this successfully for months, even though he continuously approached her when seeing her in the park. Eventually, Leslie grew weak in her fight and decided to give in to her true love.

Ms. Smiley heard rumor of her daughter's defiant behavior and she hit the ceiling with fury. She began taking Leslie to school and picking her up in the afternoons. She immediately began to scrutinize Leslie's every move when possible. Persistent about keeping Borne away from her, Borne remained persistent, as well about seeing Leslie.

The controversy grew thicker when Ms. Smiley found out that Borne had begun sneaking into her house while she was away at work.

Kim hadn't seen Leslie in a while so she dropped by one afternoon. She found Leslie and Ms. Smiley in an intense argument.

"I know that you have not been slipping that boy into my house after all we've been through. Are you crazy?"

"Someone is lying to you because I have not been sneaking Borne in your house. I do not know where you get this stuff from!" she told her mother.

"Don't you worry about where I got it from, I just know that I had better not catch that boy in my house!" Ms. Smiley turned to Kim and yelled.

"You, go home! I don't want to see your face again either Kim!"

With her head hung down, Kim walked out of Leslie's house.

"Tell your brother that I said I want him to stay away form my daughter!" she yelled at Kim.

Kim ran home to convey the message to Borne. She remained upset, confused and disappointed at Ms. Smile's scorning of her.

"Oh, I'm not thinking about that witch," Borne said.

"I know you better not go over there anymore. She was so mad. I've never seen her like that before. She even told me not to come back over there," Kim said.

That very night... Borne returned to Leslie's house... after he saw Ms. Smile's car leave. However, to his surprise when he attempted to climb through her window, Michael, Ms. Smiley's fiancé, awaited his arrival. He stood at the window.

"Borne, what is wrong with you? Do you know that I could

shoot you dead? I'm going to call the police!"

Borne went mad and grabbed the telephone from Michael's hand. They began throwing blows at one another. Borne ran down the stairs and out the front door. Michael grabbed Borne's legs and threw him on the ground. The commotion awakened most of the neighbors as they began to come out on their porches to witness the disturbance. Borne and Michael continued to fight. One of the neighbors finally called the police.

When the police arrived, they arrested Borne on the scene and charged him with breaking and entering. Michael followed them down to the police station to press assault charges against Borne for hitting him in his eye.

"What happened to your eye?" Ms. Smiley asked Michael when she returned home from work that following morning.

"I caught that Borne climbing through Leslie's window. I wanted to... I wanted to kill him!"

"Oh, I'll fix him this time!" Ms. Smiley said with determination. She stormed out of the house.

"Where are you going?" Michael asked running out the door behind her.

"To the police station, I'm going to get a restraining order out against him. He want be coming back here again!"

Ms. Smiley ran into George and Borne in the lobby of the police station. "Since you apparently can't keep that boy of yours away from my house, or my daughter, then I'm going to take further action!" she warned.

George and Borne remained speechless as they continued to walk pass her. The restraining order did keep Leslie and Borne apart for a couple of months. Borne definitely didn't try to climb back into Leslie's window.

Nothing apparently could keep the two apart as Leslie and Borne began to meet at the park once again. They began to meet at various friends' homes in the neighborhood; meeting anywhere, they felt to be discreet. The harder Ms. Smiley tried to keep them apart the more they fought to be together. It wasn't until after Leslie's third abortion that she put an end to their seven-year relationship.

Chapter 8

While Borne and Leslie were going through their problems, Jessica and Kim were hanging out together once again. They continued to pick up older men going on their joy rides. Although they found no interest what so ever in these men, they went any way. They were more concerned with what they felt these men did for their lives. These men brought life, fun and excitement to Rocking Barrel.

"Hi how are you doing today?" Jessica asked approaching a man in a red convertible. Do you feel like going for a ride and getting high?"

"Sure, get in." Jessica immediately pulled the car door open and sat in the passenger seat.

"I guess I'll see you later," Kim said.

"Where do you think you're going?" Jessica asked.

"I guess I am going home since there is only room for one of us in the car."

"Oh yeah, you're right... I guess if we both can't go then I'll get your number and call you some other time," Jessica turned towards the man and said.

He sat there with disappointment on his face, but was patient.

"Darn... I was looking forward to spending some time alone with you," he said disappointedly.

He wrote down his telephone number. "Here's my number; give me a call later and I'll come get you."

"Okay," Jessica said, as she got out of the car. He drove off down the street.

"So why didn't you go with him?"

"Oh, he was so sweet... I think I like him. I think I'll make him wait a while. Maybe I will call him later," she said.

No sooner, than he was out of their sight, another car pulled up on the curve. The driver drove up beside them and rolled down the window.

"You girls should be ashamed of your actions," the man said.

"Why is that?" Jessica asked.

"Because I've seen you here several times before stopping cars. You shouldn't be out here approaching men in this fashion," he warned. "Please be careful out here; I don't want to see anything happen to you. You know that there are some crazy people out here in this world."

His eyes now pierced Kim's eyes as he looked directly in her face.

"One day, you're going to stop the wrong car and a monster is going to be on the other side of that wheel.

You're going to get hurt out here," he insisted. He continued to stare Kim in her face as to be speaking particular to her and not Jessica.

"We're going to be just fine," Jessica, responded sarcastically. "We are big girls who know exactly what we are doing; you don't have to worry about us. What is your name any way? I haven't seen you around here before and I know everyone in town," taunting him as if he were the dangerous stranger.

"Maverick," he replied. His voice deep, but subtle... my name is Maverick," he confirmed.

Kim continued to stand there in a daze. The sight of his gorgeous face mesmerized her. He slowly began to drive away.

"That was the finest man that I have ever seen in my life. That man is going to be my husband one day," Kim stated. "Did you hear that voice? Oh, I could have just melted in his arms."

"Give it a break Kim, he really was not all that cute anyway. Now his car... that was cute."

"I'll see you later," Kim blurted out to Jessica, suddenly.

"Where are you going?"

63

"I'm going home. I'm kind of tired."

"You're... tired? Okay, I guess I'll go home and call that guy I met."

"I'll see you tomorrow." Jessica said as she headed off in the opposite direction of Kim.

Kim wasn't tired at all. She didn't want to confide to Jessica the fact that Maverick's words had wrung out to her as being true. She felt that meeting him that day was some type of sign or warning.

When she arrived home, she found the house in a peaceful state. She went into her bedroom to lie down and she focused her thoughts on Maverick. She lay there thinking about his words that weigh heavily on her heart. She considered it was best if she separate herself from Jessica who was so pompous.

So she did... Kim stayed away from Jessica for several weeks after her encounter with Maverick. Although the more she tried to stay away from her — the more Jessica urged her presence. With Jessica's telephoning her constantly she began to feel guilty about avoiding her friend. She missed her dear friend and the excitement they shared. Finally she gave into Jessica's wishes and reconsidered their friendship.

Maverick stopped to give them a ride that same afternoon that the two reunited.

"Get on in you two," he insisted. Kim could hardly believe her eyes... seeing him there in front of her.

She opened the door and lifted up the passenger seat, acknowledging to Jessica that she wished to ride in the front seat with Maverick. Although shocking to Jessica Kim's forwardness, she sat in the back of Maverick's car.

"Still on the streets I see," Maverick said sarcastically. So where would you lady's like to go this evening?" he asked with a reverent smile on his face. "Let's go across town to the tennis courts. You know the place we went the last time," Jessica suggested.

Kim sat quietly in the front seat feeling embarrassed and very confused as jealousy covered her face. She couldn't utter a word as she speculated on how the two of them ended up together at the tennis courts.

"Where was she during this encounter?" she thought.

She wouldn't dare pose the question and was glad when they finally arrived at the park.

Although it was only a five-minute trip — this day it appear to have taken an hour. So much longer to Kim as she rode in silence and disappointment. She jumped out of the car as soon as Maverick pulled into a parking space and rushed over to sit on an empty bench. Jessica and Maverick joined her and Maverick commenced to quote Bible verses. Kim was certain that this was his tactic to persuade them from hanging out on the street.

"What's wrong with you? I'm sensing that you are a little distraught," Maverick said.

"No, I'm fine." She hoped that the disappointment that she had felt earlier didn't still show upon her face. Nevertheless she thought deeply as to when and how Maverick and Jessica had spent time together without her.

Maverick sat there across from her as he continued to quote various Bible verses. Even though quite impressed by his knowledge of the Bible, she refused to indulge him in his pleasures. She stares him emotionlessly in his face as she attempt to exploit his intelligence in the area.

Why hadn't Jessica told her of their encounter, she wandered?

Jessica stood at the edge of the bench smoking one of the joints that Maverick had given to her minutes after their arrival.

"So can I light up another joint or what?" Jessica insisted, interrupting Maverick from his Bible quotes.

"Sure... have fun," he insisted.

Maverick seemed engrossed in hearing his own words. He ignored Jessica as well as the joint that she now passed back to him. As the excitement in his voice grew stronger Kim became intrigued. She felt new energy bursting through his dialogue and his heart appears sincere as he continued to enlighten them with God's word.

"You know God promises that in the last days that there will be ten women to one man," Maverick informed. "This is going to really be tough times for single women. Women will be sharing men and be glad to do so," he warned.

"I don't think so," Kim replied. "That's the one thing that I don't believe in sharing. I'll do without one, before I share one." Jessica stood there ignoring them both. Her attention stayed on the joint in which she smoked.

"You seem to know a lot about the Bible. Are you a preacher or something?"

"No, I'm no preacher. Do you honestly believe I would be sitting here smoking a joint with you two if I were?"

"I don't know. That would be between you and God. If you're not a preacher... you should be!" Kim told him. You haven't stopped talking about the Bible since we got here."

67

"I grew up with my Grandmother and she taught me many things. I used to have to go to church every Sunday." Jessica's boredom now showed all over her face.

"Well what are you guys going to do, sit here all night? Come on let's go back across town! Its boring just sitting here listening to the two of you talk about the Bible," she said. She finished the last joint.

"All right, let's go," Maverick agreed.

He didn't acknowledge the fact that Jessica had smoked his entire bag of weed and had barely shared it with him or Kim. They were so engrossed in their conversation that they hadn't realized that she had smoked it all.

The ride back home was extremely quiet. Kim sat in the back and Jessica sat in the front next to Maverick. Kim figured that since Maverick and Jessica had admitted to spending time together alone that the two might have some unfinished business. However, to her surprise, neither spoke a word as they rode in silence.

"You can let us off here," Jessica said as they arrived back to Kim's house.

She got out of the car and waited for Kim to do the same.

"Good-bye Maverick. It was nice to have seen you again. I

enjoyed our conversation and hope that we can get together again to continue it," Kim said.

"Sure, why not, I would love to finish our conversation," he said.

"What's wrong with you?" Jessica asked as Maverick drove off down the street.

"Nothing, I was just thinking about some of the things that Maverick was saying. Hey, why didn't you tell me that you and he had spent time together?"

"Well I didn't think much of it. It was a replica of today. We went to the park and I basically ignored all that talking he does as I did today. He talks entirely too much!"

Another car drove up and stopped beside of them.

"Hey, do you feel like riding out and getting high?" Jessica asked.

"Sure, get in," the man said. Kim crawled into the back seat with no hesitation and Jessica eased into the front seat.

"Hi, I'm Jessica and that's my girl, Kim."

"Hi, I'm Randy."

"So, are you going to give me a joint or what?"

"Sure, here smoke it."

Randy must have had over an ounce of marijuana. He

69

continued to hand them joint after joint, as they rode out of Rocking Barrel's city limits.

"Where are you going?" Jessica asked.

"We can't keep riding around here. I thought I would ride out of town a bit."

"Okay, just as long as we don't go too far. It would be nice to get out of Rocking Barrel for a minute," Jessica added.

"Yeah, you're right," Kim agreed. The road about thirty minutes before Kim began to feel nauseated from all the riding they had done.

"I'm feeling kind of light-headed. My head keeps on spinning, around and around. Could you please pull over Randy?" she asked.

She lay down across his back seat, curled up in a ball. Her stomach felt as though it were tied up in a knot.

"There's a store... have you eaten anything?" Randy asked.

"No, I haven't."

"I'll go in and get you something. I'm sure you'll feel much better once you've eaten something," he insisted.

"I'll get you something too Jessica," he said.

Jessica got out and went in the store with Randy. As Kim sat alone in the car her head seemed to spin around in circles.

"Here's a hamburger try to eat it," Jessica said handing Kim the burger.

"I'm ready to go home. I feel so sick," she said.
She couldn't eat the burger.

"I think I'm going to... stop the car Randy," Kim insisted.

Randy pulled over to the side of the road immediately; however, minutes too late. Kim had thrown up in the back seat of his car.

"Great!" he said sarcastically.

He looked at the mess she had made. After Kim was done Randy drove over to a nearby gas station and wiped the car down.

"I'm sorry, Randy."

"No problem... I've been there myself. I'm glad to see that you're feeling better."

He laughed at her as she lay with her head hung down on his seat.

"Kim, wake-up! Wake-up!" Jessica yelled.

Kim didn't move. She finally tapped her on her leg to awaken her.

"You're home now. I'll see you tomorrow," she said.

71

"Okay Jessica... thank you Randy," Kim said.

She could barely recognize the fact that they were parked in front of her house. Kim was so out of it that she had not thought about the fact that Jessica remained in the car with Randy. She wasn't too worried but figured that Jessica wanted to spend time with him. It wasn't often that they ran across a guy who had that much weed.

"Jessica is a tainted child and she' gotten worst since her return home. I don't want you hanging with her anymore," Joyce demanded that afternoon. "Mrs. Jerry cautioned me of the fact that she witnessed the two of you getting into some stranger's car. You're going to get in a lot of trouble hopping in and out of cars!"

Mrs. Jerry, a widow, lived down the street from Kim in a large elegant green house. She was so meddlesome. Everyone in the neighborhood disliked her because she was always interfering into their business.

"Mr. Jerry," her husband, "must have left her a fortune... she must have had a good insurance policy out on him," people would say.

Mrs. Jerry didn't do a thing all day but sit on her front porch. If she wasn't sitting out on her porch then she was peeping out the window at people as they passed by her home. In fact, Kim saw her peeping that particular day but didn't think that she saw them getting into the car. She didn't think that Mrs. Jerry even knew whom they were since when speaking to her — she never responded the neighborly gesture.

George too appeared to despise Jessica since her return home. He too forbade her from going to Jessica's home that afternoon. Kim, however, defied their wishes and continued to visit her friend. That very evening, she went to Jessica's house. That same night in which she was given her constraint she went to Jessica's house. Uncaring of the repercussions, Kim spent the evening at Jessica's home. Rebelling against her parents, she and Jessica would spend the night in hotel rooms with the fellows who had enough money to get a room. These guys who they barely knew were twice, if not three times their ages.

Although this was quite exciting for a while to Kim, it soon became a guilt trip for her. She began to speculate as to what these men wives would say had they known of their whereabouts. Even her virginity couldn't excuse her actions at this time. She felt that she was doing something dirty just by being in their presence. Unlike Jessica — she never felt guilty about anything that involved a man. More or less, Kim had become a little perturbed at her own indulgence. Feeling guilty primarily when people in the

73

neighborhood would stare at her with contempt. In particular...
Mrs. Jerry with constant bitterness in her eyes pierced through at
them and showed defiance each time they passed her home.

"Kim and Jessica, you need to leave those men alone
before you get yourselves a baby," she said to them once.

"Mind your business old lady!" Jessica replied. This
outburst embarrassed Kim somewhat.

"I'm not feeling well Jessica. I'm going to go home and get
some rest."

The next day Jessica stopped by Kim's house and George
opened the door.

"Kim Jessica's here," he said.

Jessica escorted Kim into her bedroom.

"Your father is so sexy. I sure would love to spend some
time alone with him," Jessica said.

In astonishment and total shock, Kim didn't say a word.
She never expected anyone to think such thoughts, regarding her
father, especially not her best friend.

She looked scornfully at Jessica who now appeared more
trifling than ever to her — indecent even. She could no longer
trust the stranger in whom she had become. Reality set in and as
painful as it was Kim realized that she had to let their friendship

go. She knew that this person who now stood beside her had to be a stranger. The Jessica she once loved would have never said such repulsive things regarding her father.

Chapter 9

Not long after Kim's decision to isolate herself from Jessica, her parents began discussing moving to a new neighborhood. This conversation sounded much more alluring now that Kim had broken away from Jessica.

Before Jessica's behavior change, Kim would have never thought about moving away from her old neighborhood. She loved the house, which had become somewhat apart of her. The house in which Joyce had given birth to her in she and George's bedroom. All the kids watched through the key whole to witness her birth. Even the neighborhood children were present to witness her arrival, so Kim was told.

"Joyce I think that if we move away from this neighborhood and these bad children that perhaps our children will stay out of trouble."

"I believe you're right George."

After a month of searching in Rocking Barrel, George and Joyce found a suitable new home for their family. Kim didn't want to move however she felt that it would be best if she got further away from Jessica. Adjusting for the move was very difficult for her.

Gazing around at the ceiling in her bedroom she looked around for a piece of something that she could carry with her. A concrete memory but... she found none. A deep sorrow came upon her as she begun to daydream of moving away from the only home that she had known. Although the home was quite old and run down; deserving of this look, having withstood all the bumps and bruises of twelve children.

"How could my parents possibly take me away from this house," she thought.

The house actually looked quite pleasing to her considering all the running in and out of its doors they had done. Kim was now confident that she would never forget the memories she endured while living in that house and those were enough to take with her. Living and growing up in that house was her life — her memories and the neighborhood would always be a part of her. Albeit she had calmed her thoughts... she remained confused about leaving.

George wanted them to move out of the neighborhood, not just for Kim's sake, but also because Little-Joyce was getting into trouble. She was the only sister left at home with Kim and was George's favorite daughter, named after her mother. She even looked like the senior Joyce in her younger years. She had long, shiny, silky brown hair and hazel eyes and was the splitting image of Joyce.

Little-Joyce was seeing an older guy, Gilbert, who was known and hated by everyone in town. George despised Gilbert. He was a drug dealer and user who spent time in prison. Only recently had he come home and showing no respect for his elders or any one else in the neighborhood.

The children were all overjoyed at the first sight of its brick appearance when they went to see the new home. The beautiful blossoming trees that surrounded the home as well as the neighborhood enchanted them. The house had recently been built and still held its' new home scent.

Kim would miss the old house and even its ghosts. As she stood there in the old house she reminisced back to when she saw her first spirit.

Joyce had been so tired when she came home from work that she went into the children's room to sleep. Most of the children were in her room watching television, the one black and white floor model television set that the Tuckers' owned. She sent the rest of the kids in to join them. Nicholas and Kim had gotten into a terrible fight that evening and Joyce called Kim in the room to lay down in bed next to her in the children's room.

Kim lay there listening to Joyce snore. She was not at all sleepy and wanted to go back and watch television with the other children. Suddenly, Kim felt someone lay stiffly beside of her.

"Mommy, wake up," she whispered. "Wake up mommy," she said again: but louder.

"Shut up… don't you see she's asleep?"

A man's voice wrung out in her ear. She could still hear an echo from the deep baritone sound of his voice. It was quite loud. She had never heard this voice in her house before this evening. Shockingly she turned quickly to see who lay beside her and there was no one present. She continued to view the room and remarkably still saw no visible being.

In fear she lay there with her eyes tightly shut. She didn't want to see who had spoken to her nor did she want it to speak to her again. She wonders was the voice she had heard that of the silent man — the dark man in which she had awoken to one night and many nights to follow. The man who just stood there at the door watching her as she slept.

Another encounter Kim recalled was the night when she and Little-Joyce had to sleep with Joyce because Sassy and Rosetta had come to town. They slept on Kim and Little-Joyce's bunk bed. Little-Joyce nose began to bleed in the middle of the night. Joyce pulled her out of the bed and rushed her into the bathroom.

"What's wrong?" Kim asked.

"Go back to sleep," Joyce replied.

Kim lay there in the bed with her eyes wide open awaiting their return. She hoped that the voice she had heard in the past would not speak to her in their absence. She also prayed that she not see the silent man.

As she heard Little-Joyce and Joyce coming back down the hallway, she noticed a light-toned woman smiling at her. She wore Joyce's fur coat and had long black hair, which hung down pass her shoulders. Although Kim couldn't see her shoulders through Joyce's coat, but her head and neck she could clearly see.

This coat usually hung empty on Joyce's bedroom door and since Kim could remember. The woman now hung on the door too, pinned in the coat as it hung on the hook against the door. Kim looked down to see how it could be that she hung there. She looked to see how her legs hung but to her surprise she had none.

Although the woman resembled Joyce a lot even in Kim's weariness, she knew that this was not Joyce. She appeared much too fare-skinned and her hair was a bit longer and darker than Joyce's hair.

"Look mommy," Kim yelled as her mother re-entered the room. Kim pointed excitedly at the coat and the woman in which she vividly saw. Kim never took her eyes off the woman who now disappeared in front of her and into the thin air.

"Look at what?" Joyce asked as she looked in the general area in which Kim had pointed. "Go to sleep, Kim!"

Kim closed her eyes tightly… not wanting to see the woman again. She speculated as to if Joyce had ever seen this woman.

When they awoke in the morning Kim told Joyce all about the Lady that she had seen wearing her fur coat which hung on the hook — on her bedroom door. To her surprise Joyce didn't seem shocked or in disbelief. She actually believed Kim.

"That was probably your Aunt Anna Mae, George's younger sister. She gave me that coat a year before she was murdered by her jealous lover," Joyce told. "Everyone always said that the two of us looked alike."

She couldn't bear to remember leaving the home in which she was born and therefore she chose not to remember. She quickly found herself in their new home. Gratifying to her the fact that unpacking kept her mind focused and not on the old house.

A month after settling into her new home she still had not met any one her age. She became depressed from missing her old friends. As much as she hated to admit it — she even missed Mrs. Jerry. Finding it hard to sleep at night she welcomed a visit from any one… even the ghosts from the old house. At least she wouldn't be so alone. She watched her bedroom door frequently to see if maybe her tall dark ghost friend would come to visit her. The one who never said a word and had no face. Yes the silent man — the dark man. She only saw his pearly white teeth as he often stood watching her as she slept.

She even welcomed the ghost who scared all the Tucker children out of their house one afternoon. He kept knocking on the closet wall in their bedroom as they play. This was the closet that they often taunted one another about the ghost being and living in, however no one believed it until this day.

"Come out… come out and show your face," they all taunted that afternoon. The sheet that hung over the door to cover its appearance flew forcefully back as if someone held it open tightly. They all ran out of the house and down the street to the liquor house where Joyce was sitting. They told her what had happened; however, when they returned to the house he didn't show his face.

Kim was so lonely in the new home that she welcomed the ghost. She wished someone would have come to visit her but no one showed. Not even the ghost from her old home. Borne and Leslie walked into the house one afternoon when Kim was sitting around watching television.

"Why don't you come to the park any more Kim?" Leslie asked.

"I don't want to walk there by myself. Borne and Nicholas always leave the house so early and before I've gotten dressed."

"Perhaps you could ask your father to drop you off on his way to work," Leslie suggested.

Kim decided to take her up on her advice and asked George to drop her off at the park that following day. She also arranged for her father to pick her up on his way home from work. After a month of George dropping her off and picking her up from the park, Kim finally began to walk there on her own. She would run briskly through the wooded shortcut areas in which Borne and Leslie had shown her.

She was quite happy that following Christmas, when George purchased her a bicycle. Jessica also had gotten a bike and would meet Kim halfway. Yes, she had forgiven her friend and no longer condemned her for her actions. Although she

83

strongly felt that Jessica should be more discreet in soliciting her men.

Jessica was now seeing Keith, a thirty-five-year-old man. Jessica had only recently turned fourteen. She thought this was an excellent thing in life and constantly tried to match her up with his friends. Kim repeatedly refused them, upsetting Jessica. She truly felt that Keith and his friends were too old for them to be enjoying her and Jessica's company. She had no interest in them at all, but more so in the younger guys in her age group.

Keith was very attractive and Kim admired his gorgeous olive green eyes. She sympathized with Jessica in knowing how they could mesmerize her. He and Jessica looked so good together. They appeared to be the perfect couple — not considering their age difference.

Keith did everything possible to keep Jessica happy, during the three months that they dated. However, nothing he did was good enough for her. Naturally, she was never satisfied. She always expected more than some would say she deserve. Soon she became bored with Keith too and she began to mess around with other men.

The majority of the guys she cheated on him with were married. Keith became so fed up with her running around on him an ignoring him that he broke up with her. Only a week had passed since their break up and already Jessica had her mindset on someone else.

"You have got to come see this guy who just moved next door to me. He is so fine. Come with me home and I'll call him so that you can meet him. That's if his wife isn't home," she admitted.

Kim was aware of the fact that he too was married even before Jessica mentioned it. She agreed to go with Jessica to meet him. Immediately after arriving there, Jessica picked up the telephone and invited herself over to his house.

"Pete, is it okay if my girlfriend and I come over to your house?"

She quickly hung up the telephone and grabbed Kim by her arm, pulling her madly out the door. It was obvious to Kim from her enthusiasm and the huge smile on Jessica's face that Pete had agreed to let them come over.

As they approached his porch, Kim saw his silhouette on the screen door. He was too handsome. Once meeting him, she too felt that she even could have fallen for him. She admitted to Jessica that she had nice taste in men. Even though she thought it was impossible to compare Keith as far as attractiveness, other than his eyes. Pete remained blessed and was far better looking than any of Jessica's ex-boyfriends. He stood there with bulging upper arms through his navy blue sweatshirt in which he wore. His navy blue swim trunks matched every bulge. Kim found him to be an even bigger flirt than Jessica as he eyed her up and down. His tongue appears to hang out of his mouth. She found it very hard to believe that he was actually married.

He and Jessica began to kiss as soon as they entered the house. Jessica gave a quick introduction as they strolled down a long narrow corridor to his bedroom. Kim sat on the sofa with Carl, whom Pete had also introduced briefly. She and Carl made small talk trying not to listen to the bumping and moaning they surely heard coming from the bedroom.

Pete, finally opened the bedroom door. As he and Jessica started down the corridor Kim heard Genie, Jessica's sister, approaching the porch. In desperation and fear of Genie catching them there, she crawled across the door and into the hallway on her hands and knees. She instructed Pete and Jessica to get back into the bedroom.

"Genie's coming to the door," she whispered.

She hoped that the covered screen door had successfully hidden her silhouette from her.

86

Jessica and Kim entered Pete's bedroom as he went down the corridor into the front room where he greeted Genie at the door. The girls remained in the bedroom behind the closed door.

As they sat there Kim admired the elegant peach satin sheets on the bed and the silk thick plush comforter with matching shams. The comforter was slightly folded back. She looked across the room at the peach satin curtains that matched perfectly with the bedding. She wanted to touch the curtains to see if they too were indeed satin: but she didn't. She admired Pete and his wife Karen's bedroom: the gold-framed mirrors on the ceiling, the white candles that stood tall in their peach candleholders on each cherry wood nightstand. Their wedding picture that hung so eloquently over the cherry wood headboard also framed in gold.

"Hello Pete... is Karen home?" Genie asked.

"No, she hasn't returned home from work."

"Well, tell her I stopped by to see her. You don't have any weed do you?"

"No, not at this time."

When Kim and Jessica heard Genie's footsteps leaving the porch, they came quietly down the corridor and joined Pete and Carl. They sat with them on the sofa. Pete had closed the front door. The four of them sat there comfortably for hours, getting high. Kim and Jessica then left Pete's house and only minutes before Karen was to return home from work.

Although Kim remained afraid to the fact that Karen could come home at any moment to catch them there, she didn't let her fear show. She too sat calmly and relaxed along side Jessica, Carl and Pete.

"Jessica, weren't you at all concerned at the fact that Karen could come home at any moment to find you lying in her bed with her husband?" Kim asked.

"No, I've been watching her leave out in the mornings. I have her schedule timed perfectly."

"I was so scared when Genie came over. I thought that it was Karen. I could hardly breathe. I definitely want be going there anymore," Kim admitted.

"I like being alone anyway, especially when it comes to making love. I just wanted you to see how fine he is girl."

She knew that if they had been caught that Pete and Jessica would have come up with some reasoning as to why they were there. Jessica was great at getting out of these types of situations.

Kim thought about how pretty Karen looked in her wedding pictures... like a princess. She knew that Jessica had not thought twice about the picture. She probably didn't notice it at all.

One of the neighbors who had seen the activity at Pete's house that afternoon informed Karen that they had been there. She also told her that Jessica had been coming to her home while she was at work. Karen went immediately to Jessica's home that afternoon she was informed and confronted her. She sought the truth to the rumor as well as an explanation as to why Jessica and Kim were at her house that day. She also wished to know why Jessica was there those other days.

"I heard that you have been spending time at my home while I'm at work... Is this true?"

"Yeah I've been over your house maybe once or twice while you were at work," Jessica, answered without fear. "We were just sitting over there getting high," she added.

"We... who is we?" Karen asked.

"Me and my girlfriend Kim," Jessica told.

"I would appreciate it if you would stay away from my husband and my home, especially when I'm not there!" Karen informed her forcefully.

"What's going on in here Karen?" Genie asked having entered the room.

"Your sister has just confessed to spending time with my

husband while I am away at work. I've asked that she not come over to my house when I'm not there," Karen said.

"Is that all? I went over there myself, today," Genie told. "Jessica, when were you over there?"

"I don't know what time it was," she said. I've been over there several of times. Kim and I went over and smoked a joint earlier today," she admitted. "Now that I see it's such a problem... then I won't be going back over there!"

Jessica had, once again, maneuvered her way out of being caught having an affair with someone's husband. She stood there looking and appearing to be so innocent looking Karen directly in her face. Two months following this incident Karen and Pete moved out of the neighborhood.

The house remained vacant for a month before Charles and his wife, Lydia, moved into it. Charles was a tall, brown skinned man. He had a full beard that flickered with gray, which satisfied Jessica's desires. Of course, he too was quite handsome. The wrinkles underneath and around his eyes told of his age. He appeared to be in his early forties. Jessica's eyes gleamed aimlessly at him, as she sat on her front porch watching him and his pregnant wife move their belongings into the house.

Jessica began to prey on him that very afternoon. Even as

he and his wife commenced to move into their new house. The fact that Lydia was in her fifth month of pregnancy was not at all relevant to Jessica. Jessica's only concern was her appetite for Charles.

Three weeks later, after the coupled settled into their new home, Jessica and Charles became further acquainted. A week later, they were sneaking off to one of the hotels in Rocking Barrel. Neither Jessica, nor Charles had any shame or morals.

Kim wonders now about her morals as she stood there in his living room staring him in his face.

Charles and Jessica dated for months. Everyone in the neighborhood was aware of this fact, of course, except for Lydia. No one wanted to be the bearer of bad news in consideration of the baby she carried.

The two continued their affair up until the day Lydia came home from the hospital with her son in her arms. After arriving home, full with excitement to have her son, Lydia went in her house. She laid her baby boy down securely in his crib and she came to pay Jessica a surprise visit.

"Hello, you're Jessica, aren't you?" she asked.

"Yes, I'm Jessica.

Lydia grabbed Jessica by the shirt and then by her hair.

She then dragged her out of the house by her hair out into the street. She had somehow found out about the affair. Jessica had always counted on Genie to fight her battles for her. However this time Genie was nowhere to be found.

Relentlessly Lydia and Jessica fought up and down the street. No one came to Jessica' aide, or to her defense, as the battle continued to its end. This was only when Charles finally came home from work and saw the two struggling. It didn't take long for him to figure out that it was his own wife and Jessica who fought that evening. He parked his car immediately on the side of the road and ran to break up the fight. He picked Lydia up and took her into the house.

Although Jessica came to Kim's house to tell her of the encounter, the news had already sprung out through Rocking Barrel. Everyone in town talked about the violent fight that day.

"I'm sorry that she found out about the two of you Jessica. You must have known that she would find out eventually. Besides, you were completely wrong in seeing Charles."

"How could you say these things to me Kim? You're my friend and I thought that friends were supposed to stick together!"

"You are my friend Jessica, however I'm embarrassed by the way you manipulate these men. Certainly, you can get their attention. You're giving them what they want and free of charge. Why can't you see that they are simply taking advantage of you? They're not going to leave their wives for you? Besides, how would you like it if it were your husband having an affair on you?"

"I don't expect them to leave their wives for me! I'm never going to get married, so I'm not concerned about anyone sleeping with my husband."

"At the rate you're going... you're right. You want have a husband. No one will want to marry you."

Becoming frustrated with Kim's attitude Jessica walked away — without saying good-bye. Kim stood there... unsure as to why she had said all those hurtful things to her friend.

"Was it because of what she was doing or because her parents were pressuring her to stay away from Jessica," she thought.

"You hang out one more night and we're going to put you in a girl's home," George and Joyce threatened again.

Minutes later Jessica showed up at the door.

Her parents blamed Jessica for her staying out all night. Kim however faulted Felicia for her shortcoming. There was no doubt in her mind regarding the fact that her parent's would indeed send her away from home.

93

Chapter 10

Unexpectedly Felicia returned home from Washington, DC after having a nervous breakdown. At least this is what Sassy, whom she had been living with for the past 7 years explained had happened to Felicia. The doctors however diagnosed her with being paranoid schizophrenic. They also confirmed that she had been born with this mental malfunction.

Having settled back home in as little as two weeks Felicia merely sat around the house. When she first arrived to town she would sit in her bedroom — talking aloud to herself. Eventually she moved out in the living room where she would do the same. She constantly insisted that bugs and other inanimate creatures crawled around in her bedroom at night. Relentlessly she persisted that rats ran freely throughout her body... impregnating her. If she wasn't talking irrational to herself then she was making death threats to Kim.

"I'm going to kill you bitch... go to sleep! I can't wait until you go to sleep," she would threaten.

Constantly Kim tried to explain to her parents the insane things that Felicia would say to her at night. They however refused to believe her. They also refused to face the fact that

Felicia was madly insane. Instead of listening to Kim's concerns, they would accuse her of exaggerating the truth. They brushed away the seriousness of Felicia's death threats as being a fear tactic.

"Felicia is not going to harm you," they insisted — although they remained locked away in their bedroom at night.

Borne and Nicholas too lay behind their locked door each night as Kim remained alone with nowhere to run. It was as though she were losing her sanity and yet... no one nurtured her wounds. It appeared that no one cared about her safety since she received no help from her parents or siblings in protecting her from Felicia.

Kim wanted so to get out of the house away from them all but there it was she had once again turned away from Jessica. She had run off her only friend — after her confrontation with Lydia.

How could it be that she now questioned her decisions? *"How could she end their friendship,"* she thought.

Although Kim had stayed away from Jessica's house she continued to come by weekly. Kim however offered no compromise, which finally ran Jessica away for what she had hoped would be an eternity. Now here she sat wanting her dear friend.

Finally on a Sunday evening Jessica came by wanting Kim to come meet another one of her new men friends. Kim was glad to see Jessica who couldn't have come at a more opportune time.

"Kim come and meet my new friend," Jessica said. She was so excited.

"Okay Jessica but I can only stay for a short time. I have to study for a test that I have tomorrow."

In some essence she felt as if she were only using Jessica to get away from Felicia.

"Bring your books and I'll help you study," Jessica suggested.

She ran back out to the car where her friend sat waiting patiently and Kim followed with her books in her hands. Although she wondered how Jessica with her tenth grade education could possibly help her study.

"James this is my girlfriend Kim that I have been telling you about," she said.

Kim sat flamboyantly in his white Cadillac that had baby blue leather interior. It appeared to drown her as she sank downward in the plush seats.

They arrived at Jessica's house where James dropped them off.

96

"Be back at ten o'clock," Jessica yelled to him as he drove away.

They went into the house and sat as Kim began to study Jessica turned on the radio to listen to the slow tunes... as she did so often. Having finished studying for her test Kim became extremely bothered at the fact that James had not returned. She glanced at the clock on the wall and saw that it was ten-thirty.

"Do you think James heard you when you said to be back by ten-o'clock? My parents are going to kill me! They said that if I wasn't back by eleven o'clock that they were going to put me in a girl's home," she told.

"You should have told me that before he left so that I could have explained that to him. I'm sure he would have come back on time if he had known. Don't worry he'll be here soon," Jessica insisted.

Eleven o'clock came and James still had not returned and Kim was even more concerned about making her curfew.

"What am I going to do?"

"I don't know Kim... let's go up the road to Mr. Grip's house. There's usually someone over there. I'm certain we can find you a ride home."

Mr. Grip owned the biggest liquor house in town. This is

where all the men would go to have drinks and play cards. Twenty to thirty men and women sat around inside the home purchasing drinks and gambling. However this night: out of all nights, no one came out to the liquor house. In disappointment they walked back towards Jessica's house. As they strolled onward they viewed car lights approaching from behind. The lights shined against the leaves on the trees that faced them. It pulled slowly up beside them and stopped.

"Hello Tucker and Barber," the driver said. He seemed to know them by names, their last names.

"Do you know us?" Kim asked.

"Sure, I do... don't you remember me? I am Nichol's brother Jason."

Kim desperately tried to place his face however she couldn't recall seeing him before that evening.

"Sure, I remember you Jason. So how is your sister Nichol doing? Do you think you could give my girlfriend Kim a ride home? She was supposed to have been home by ten-thirty," Jessica informed.

"Where does she live?"

"In Claritin Woods."

They continued to talk across her as if she weren't there. Kim stood in silence as Jessica made plans for her — as usually.

"No problem... get in," he said looking hungrily at Kim. "I live not too far from there," he added.

"Get his tag number," Kim whispered to Jessica as she got into the car.

For some reason she just didn't like the dark mysterious look in Jason's eyes. Nor did she like the devious grin he held upon his face. He drove away slowly and made small talk along the way.

Kim thought about the gratified look that Jessica had as she walked towards her house. She appeared relieved and at ease that Kim had finally gotten a ride home.

"I know you remember me Kim," Jason said. "Don't you remember me?"

"I think I do remember meeting you before," Kim said shyly. Yes now that I think about it, I do," Kim said. Although she remained certain that she had never met Jason before Kim went along with his persistence in having met her before.

"I certainly remember your pretty face. I will never forget that night when we were over Nichol's house playing cards. You're quite a card player too... if I recall correctly."

"You must be talking about one of my sisters," Kim suggested. "I've never been over to Nichol's house."

Jason didn't respond but only laughed in disbelief. As they were approaching a four-way stoplight Kim noticed that Jason had turned on his turning signal.

"You're to keep straight to get to my house. I thought you said you knew where I lived."

"I know where you live but I just thought that you would like to go to my home for a few night caps before going home," he coached.

"No thank you Jason. I really need to get home. I'm already an hour late."

Jason never took his signal off as he cleared the green light continuing into a left turn. Kim opened the passenger's door in an effort to hop out of the car. As she opened the door Jason sped up his car turning the car so rapidly that Kim's door almost closed on her leg.

"I told you that I didn't want to go to your house Jason! You stop this car and let me out... right now!" she demanded.

"I have to go to my house to pick up something. Just calm down," he insisted. "I promise to take you straight home afterwards."

"No just let me out right here and I'll walk! I'm sure that whatever you have to get from your house can wait until after you have taken me home. My house is right up the street. Pull over and let me walk!" Kim pleaded forcefully however he continued to ignore her. He drove onward through a long dark tunnel.

"Where are you going?"

"Calm down. My house is just to the right of here."

They turned down a long dark dirt road that appeared to never end. Kim was furious and somewhat fearful of Jason's actions. She looked out the window to the left and to the right of her trying to see where he was taking her. She prayed to see a home or a store — anything, but there was nothing. There were only woods in Jason's domain. Although he drove slower... she was still frightened. It was so dark and appeared to get even darker as he drove deeper into the wooded area. Even the darkness didn't detour him as he continued on his mission to get down the dirt road. He finally turned to the right bearing off the long dirt road. Before reaching its end Kim noticed a white house. She felt relieved and confident that there would be someone inside who would help her get home.

Who could live out here alone? she thought.

Jason pulled his car around to the back of the house. As he parked the car Kim realized that this was Jason's big white house. She sat wondering if she should get out of the car and run for the tunnel. The thought of going back up that long dark dirt road frightened her even more than Jason frightened her.

"Come on in — I'm not going to bite. I'm sure that you don't want to sit out here in the dark and by yourself."

"No I don't mind sitting out here. It's no problem. Go ahead inside and get what ever it is you need to get. I'll be here when you return," she said.

Jason got out of the car and came around to the passenger side of the car where she sat silently. He opened the door.

"Get out," he said calmly.

"No I told you I'll wait here."

Kim assumed that he came around to try to talk her into coming in the house. However Jason had other plans. He grabbed her up out of the seat and across the yard.

"Put me down! What is wrong with you? I told you that I didn't want to go in there! Put me down Jason!"

She yelled continuously while kicking and hitting him forcefully. He threw her across his shoulder and continued to drag her towards his house.

"Come on... stop fighting me! Let's go in here and have some fun."

"What do you mean... have fun? I don't want to have fun

with you! Please just take me home!" she pleaded.

When he reached his back door he put his key in the door with one hand and held Kim tightly with the other. Jason was quite a huge man about six feet tall and 190 pounds... too much of a match for Kim. As he opened the door he continued to hold her across his shoulder and with ease. Jason was no match for Kim who could only cry after having put up a good fight that evening.

Chapter 11

Once Jason entered the house, he placed Kim gently down on his shoulder. Her feet now touched the floor. She stood there looking around and exploring his surrounding. The house was dark. Drafty winds rushed suddenly pass her causing a cold chill to run up her spine. She could smell the dampness coming through the walls of the house. As she scrutinized his house, she eyed ragged furniture in the kitchen as well as in the living room.

"Come on in here and sit with me," Jason said calmly.

Kim had not realized that he had left out of the kitchen or that he had closed and locked the door behind her. Looking back at the door, Kim noticed three dead bolts secure the door shut.

"Be nice and he'll take me home... he is obviously high," she thought.

She began to pray to God to keep her safe from Jason's wrath.

"Do you live here alone?"

She entered the living room that appeared to be his bedroom also. He lay arrogantly across the bed. Kim sat down on the sofa and he got up to turn on a dim dark blue light. Trying to hold her composure and appear less edgy she began to participate in his dialogue.

"Yes I do live here alone."

"You have a cozy little place here. So did you get what you came inside to get?" she asked. She didn't want her fear to show.

"What did you say to me?"

"Get what you came to get so that we can go," she continued.

"I know you're not rushing me."

"No, it's... I know my parents are worried sick about me. I was supposed to be home before ten-thirty. What time is it now?"

"Twelve-thirty," he said.

He pointed to the clock on the wall.

"They've probably called the police."

"Wouldn't you like a drink?" he asked.

"No thank you Jason. I would really like to go home."

"Have a seat! Relax... you're making me nervous."

"How can I relax when I need to get home?"

"I guess I'm a lot like Freddie."

"Freddie, who's Freddie?"

"Freddie's my twin brother. He's really sick you know. We had to have him institutionalized but he'll be out soon."

Kim got paranoid thinking that perhaps Jason was not Jason but instead perhaps: Freddie. The more he talked the more frightened she became. Kim now fears for her life.

"Would you please... please take me home?"

"I will take you home. I promised you I would. I just need someone to talk to so relax. I will take you home just be patient."

He continued to talk about Freddie. "Everyone said that I was the bad twin and that Freddie was the good one. Look at us now... I'm here and he's locked up like some kind of animal."

He got up off the bed and moved rapidly over to the sofa towards where Kim sat. Her heart began to pound anxiously. Frightened by his sudden movement towards her she clinched her hands in a tight fist. He sat down next to her. His face... intolerable — filled with acne and lesions. He was very unattractive. Kim in her madness thought him to be quite ugly. He put his arm around her and leaned over towards her as he attempted to give her a kiss on her lips. She quickly turned her head to the side to avoid their lips meeting. She pushed him away vigorously with her hands.

"What do you think you're doing?"

"Come on, stop fighting me. You know you want me as much as I want you."

Pulling her closer to him forcefully, he slid himself towards the end of the sofa.

"Oh, you think you are too good for me. Is that what this is?"

As Kim fought to get away from his sexual advancements, he reached his long arms over her shoulder tearing her blouse from the front. She continued to push him away.

"What have you done? My mother is going to kill me!"

"Stop trying to act as if you are a good girl! Little girls like you come a dime a dozen."

Kim started to cry as he began rubbing himself all over her breast. She fought him with all of her strength. He grabbed her off the sofa and threw her onto his bed.

"Please Jason... don't hurt me!"

Jason said nothing however he continued to kiss her on her neck, face and down the sides of her neck. She lay there crying, screaming and pleading with him not to hurt her. Reaching one hand down her shirt and unzipping her pants with the other he began to whisper to her, "I love you."

Kim began to fight him with all her might and this seemed to make it easier for him to maneuver her pants down. As he leaned down to take her pants off Kim kicked him in his face. This made him angry. He now became violent as he balled up his fist to hit her in the face. She was relieved that he didn't hit her with his fist. He slapped her instead. Her face began to swell.

"I'm a virgin, Jason and I don't want to have sex with you! Please stop."

"You are a little liar. You're not a virgin. They don't exist anymore. They went out with the fifties."

He laughed hysterically and continued to pull her panties down. Kim began to cry and scream louder and louder.

"Go ahead and scream, no one can hear you. You are going to make me hurt you if you continue to fight me. I don't want to have to hurt you, so stop fighting me and just relax! It will be over before you know it... daddy's going to make you feel better. Just stop your crying!"

She lay feeling dirty and helpless while staring at the ceiling. She prayed to God — "Dear God, could you please end my torment quickly. Please do not let Jason hurt me. Am I deserving of this madness?"

She prayed aloud as Jason uncaringly continued to penetrate her. As his penis went in and out of her, his sweat poured continuously onto her body.

"How could you allow this to continue, dear Lord?" she prayed.

"Say it, say you love me!"

Kim didn't respond, however, she continued to lie there as he restrains her tightly down on the bed. She would die before she'd tell him she loved him.

What had she done? Was it something that she had once said in her life that could cause her to be going through this night with Jason? Was there some type of lesson to be learned from all this misery? How could he dare lay there on top of her violating her and telling her how great she was to him?

Her mind thinks back to all the bad things that she had done in her life. Filled with many questions, she could find only one answer to that question. She had defied her parents, constantly by staying out all night. She should have listened to her parents and come home on time.

"It feels good... say it is good!" he so arrogantly demanded. "I know you want it. Say it now... I got to hear it. Tell it to me woman!"

Kim lay there like a rock. She had no movement, no sounds and no feeling to offer him. As he inserted his penis in and out of her, she became sicker and sicker. She had no sexual feeling at all. All she felt was unadulterated numbness.

Kim wanted Jason off her more than ever but he kept on

penetrating her. It was as though someone was beating a drum in her ear and she wanted the music to stop banging so loud. She thought the music would never stop and that Jason would never tire. She felt as if she had died and gone to hell. Jason was Satan and the fire burned through to her soul!

"It feels good... it does, it feels really good." Jason roared. "Say it! Say it feels good!"

It was worse enough that she had to lay there and go through this torment. Now for him to have the audacity to insist that she play a part in his madness was pure cruelty. Kim refused to play a script in his play. Therefore, she said nothing. He didn't feel good to her — Jason didn't feel good at all! Lying there numb, with him between her legs, Kim felt nothing. Her mind and spirit floated away from her body that remain limp. She lay there senselessly with nothing to give him; comatose she lay there up on Jason's bed as he continue to take her person.

Kim looked above her head and remarkably she sees her spirit floating above Jason's body.

She laughs as a since of peace now comes to save her. Her spirit took over her every being. She now watches Jason from above and through her spirits' eyes. As her spirit floats above him the fear relinquishes from within her. This once so big man no longer appears to be such a big figure. On the contrary; he appears quite minute, weak.

"I hate you! You act like some mad dog: attacking me in this manner! Get up! Get off of me!"

"I bet you come back for more of this dog!" he said. He kept penetrating her as her spirit now returned to her in its completeness.

She lay there a minute longer watching the hands on the clock go around and around ceaselessly.

"How much longer can he go?" she thought.

She was so exhausted… yet he had so much energy. She continued to watch the hands on the clock go from two-thirty To four o'clock. He continued to penetrate her insides with force.

"How much longer can he go?" she thought.

She was so exhausted. He had so much energy. She continued to watch the hands on the clock go from two-thirty to four o'clock. He continued to penetrate her insides with force.

"Would he ever stop?" she wondered.

All her praying, crying and Jason's penetration had exhausted her to the point where she could no longer stay awake. She felt so weak and so tired. She leaves the room once more. This time her Spirit leaves her body and floats above Jason. She watches it — her Spirit — as it watches her. She appears to be in a pleasant sleep. She slept until five-thirty when she awakened to find her spirit reuniting sequentially with her body. Jason still lay on top of her pounding away at her insides. She didn't know if he had taken a break during the time she had been away in her spirit rim or not. Although she did recall her dream of being safely home in her bed.

With renewed energy inside of her now she felt strong minded and full of will power. So much so that she began kicking and screaming. She fought him vigorously and like a salmon struggling onward upstream. Forcefully she managed to kick him off her and onto the floor. She dived down on the floor on top of him. Shocked to see that she had so much energy — she hit him in the head and any part of his body that she could reach. She was no longer afraid. It was as though she was someone else… the way she hit Jason with such a strong force of powerful energy.

"I want to go home! Take me home! I'm sick of you!"

She cried frantically as she continued to beat him.

"Okay put your clothes on and I'll take you home now," he succumb.

Kim could see distinct fear in Jason's eyes for the first time that night. He had exhausted himself to where he now couldn't fight back. She released him relieved that he would be really taking her home where she broke down into tears. Truly, he had to mean it this time and she was going home. Kim began to put her clothes on as he did the same from the other side of the room.

Albeit she felt dirty and ashamed. Nevertheless she was thankful to be going home. She still felt hatred inside for Jason and she wanted revenge. Above all, she wanted to get in her bed and go to sleep. She trusts that her dreams still brought reassurance and delight.

Kim tried to walk for the first time and noticed that she could barely move her legs. Jason pushed her toward the bedroom door, she saw an opened pocketknife on the bookshelf. Kim stopped in her track. It was at arm's reach for her. They now walked out the door. She had not seen it earlier.

With Jason's back now facing her, she grabbed the knife and stabbed him forcefully in the back. Strangely enough Jason never fell. Instead, he continued to walk boldly onward as Kim now looked down at her hand. The knife was no longer there.

"Why is he still walking and why has he not fallen, she thought?"

Kim turned her head and clearly saw that the knife remained seated on the shelf. She had not stabbed him. It had been only a figment of her imagination.

"Had she gone mad? Had her anger taken possession of her?" Although she wanted to grab the knife to kill him — something deep inside of her wouldn't allow her to commit murder.

She could barely walk though she continued out the door behind him as she embraced the wall. With each step she found it hard to maneuver. Jason was in the car blowing his horn impatiently.

"Hurry up or you will be walking back to town!" he urged.

Kim tried to increase her pace as he blew the horn forcefully. She sat down in the front seat and began to cry as he drove madly back down the dirt road. He drove through the dark tunnel onto the main street.

"Shut up! Stop crying! You want to get put out don't you!" he threatened.

Kim closed her eyes and began to mumble underneath her breath, "you bastard."

She didn't want to irritate him. He stopped the car.

"Get out!" he demanded.

"Please... no, don't put me out of the car," she begged.

"Get out... you're here!" he said.

Kim looked over and saw that she was back at Jessica's house. After all the torment that he had put her through he still refused to take her home.

"I thought that you were taking me home."

"Get out or I'll take you back home with me."

"Please take me home. I don't want them to see me like this. Why can you not just drop me off in front of my house?"

"Get out!"

He reached over and opening the passenger's door and pushed her onto the concrete pavement. He drove away.

Chapter 12

Kim didn't look back. She crawled up the sidewalk as she tried to stand but couldn't. She could only get up on her knees. She crawled slowly up the pathway that led to the steps of Jessica's house. As she approached the steps she began to cry. She wondered how she could possibly climb them. She rested her head at the edge of the bottom step where she lay sobbing. Finally, she regained enough energy to crawl up a few steps. Half way up the steps she realized that she didn't have the energy to continue her effort to reach the door to house. She rested once more at the top of the steps until she was able to gain more energy. Finally she crawled up onto the porch and ultimately she was at Jessica's door.

She tapped softly but as hard as she could on the door. There was no answer. Her strength failed her once again and she had no strength left in her to knock harder. Given up all hope she lay lifelessly drowning in her tears.

"Who's there?" Mr. Barber asked. He opened the door to find Kim lying there on his porch.

"Kim, is that you? Why are you here at my door this time of the morning?"

Kim couldn't speak. Mr. Barber picked her up from off of the porch and brought her inside. He helped her into the den where he laid her down on the sofa. He left her and ran into Jessica's bedroom to implore her to Kim's aide.

"Wake-up Jessica, wake-up!" he said frantically.

"What's wrong daddy?" Genie asked.

"Kim's in the living room crying hysterically. I am trying to wake Jessica to see what is wrong with her. She's crying and can barely stand."

Genie came into the den where Kim laid on the sofa. "What's wrong with you Kim?"

Kim opened her eyes for a second and tried to speak but no words came out of her mouth. Only tears ran down her face. Tammy came running out along with Mr. Barber. They all stood there trying to find out why Kim had come to their home at six thirty in the morning barely in touch with her surroundings.

Jessica finally came out to see her friend lying helplessly on the sofa.

"What in the world is Kim doing back here? Oh my God," she cried. Kim knew from those words that Jessica knew what had happened. She knew from the look on Kim's face and her torn clothes she still wore that were ripped from her body. She

117

knew that Jason had kept her out all night and had not taken her home as he promised. She looked at her friend who lay with her blouse ripped.

"What's going on Jessica?" Mr. Barber asked.

"Kim left here last night with Jason, Nichol's brother. He was supposed to have given her a ride home."

"The crazy one?" Genie asked.

"No, not him... his twin. How do you know it wasn't the crazy one?" Tammy urged.

"Who is Jason?" Mr. Barber asked.

"You remember Nichol, she comes over to play cards on the weekends, daddy. It's one of her brothers," Genie continued.

"Oh yeah, I remember Nichol. I don't think I've met her brothers. Have they been over too?"

"No, they have never been over."

That is the last thing Kim heard and remembered before falling asleep. Her eyes felt like bags of sand. She slept for hours and when she awoke it was two o'clock. She found all the bad memories remained embedded in her brain. Jessica and her family along with James sat patiently in the den waiting for Kim to awake.

"Where was James last night and why did he not come back to take her home as he promised?" she thought.

"Are you okay now?" Jessica asked.

"I'll never be okay again."

"What happened?"

"I don't want to talk about it right now," Kim replied. She knew that they were worried about her, but she didn't yet have the energy to reveal the event in detail.

"I just want to take a bath," she moaned. Jessica grabbed Kim by her hand and led her gently into the bathroom.

"Have a seat and I'll fix you a bath."

As Jessica cleaned the tub and prepared Kim's bath, she and Jessica both stared in silence. Kim lay back in the tub for hours. She tried desperately to wash Jason away. She was glad that no one bothered her and that the Barbers' let her take her time to prepare to confront her parents.

Kim had always felt at home at Jessica's house and even more now but she knew that eventually the time would come when she would have to go home to face her parents. She sensed that perhaps her parents were somehow already aware of the torture that she had endured while captured in Jason's unpitying web.

119

"Why then did she have to confirm her hurt and embarrassment by confirming their fears to be true?" she thought.

She didn't want to see the disappointing looks on their faces. She wished that she could stay at Jessica's house forever and never had to go home to confront her parents. In all reality, she knew that this was impossible.

"I think you should go home and talk to your parents. I'm sure that they are worried sick about you," Mr. Barber said. Kim was now facing the reality she dreaded.

"Joyce is going to kill her when she gets home daddy," Jessica promised.

"She surely will. Please don't make me go there, not yet! This would have never happened, if I had stayed at home, as my parents warned me. Please don't tell them! You cannot tell my parents what happened! I don't want anyone to know!" Kim pleaded.

"We will not tell them, if that's what you prefer," Genie said.

Kim knew deep inside there was no way they could keep it a secret from her family.

"Let us take you home," Genie insisted.

Kim followed Genie out of the door and joined James and Jessie in the car. She slept all the way home. She continued to feel as though she had been beat with a whip all night.

When they arrived at Kim's house, no one bothered to wake her.

"We'll go in and talk to her parents to see if we can sooth the situation. She has already been through enough," Kim overheard Genie whisper.

Although Kim could hear Genie's words, she was unable to open her eyes to speak. She heard them get out of the car and imagined their going inside her house. Knowing that it was better that she remain behind, because she didn't have the heart or energy to tell her parents what had happened. Just the thought of entering her home brought emotions of a nervous breakdown.

Kim at last opened her eyes but didn't have the nerves to go inside the house. It seemed that hours had past since the others had entered the house. She didn't want to face her parents... not yet. She sat nervously out in the car as she imagined what could be going on inside. The more she tried to picture her mother's response, the more she wanted to join them in the house. Her legs still would not move. Shortly thereafter, she noticed Jessie and James coming towards the car.

"How did they take it?" she asked as Jessica opened the door. "Did they say that they were going to put me in a girl's home?"

"No Kim. They seemed to be really concerned about you," James said.

"Come on in. They want to talk to you," Jessica said. Kim got out of the car and followed James and Jessica back inside. Her legs seemed to wobble and shake like jelly as she neared the door.

"I knew something was wrong," Joyce said as Kim entered the door. "I couldn't sleep all night. So tell me Kim what happened?"

Kim stood baffled and didn't say a word. She didn't want to discuss the rape. Once again, she opened her mouth but couldn't speak. She tried to hold back her tears but she couldn't. She ran breathlessly into her room where Felicia lay quietly and she locked the door. She hoped that her mother would not follow.

Even Felicia could tell that something was obviously wrong with Kim, who was not her normal self. Felicia left the room and joined the others out in the living room where they discussed Kim's ordeal.

As Kim lay there in the bedroom, she overheard Jessica telling her parents what had happened. She tried desperately to answer all of their questions and finally heard Jessica say good-bye. Kim knew that she was now alone with her parents, as things began to quiet down. Kim dosed off to sleep. She awoke to her mother screaming out, "You whore!"

Kim didn't know what her mother's screams were about or how long she had been screaming.

"Shush... Joyce. She's trying to get some sleep," George said.

"You know she's lying. No one raped her! She's just been hanging out again with that whore, Jessica!"

It was obvious to Kim from the tone of Joyce's voice that she had been drinking and therefore she remained in her bedroom, she hoped to avoid Joyce's wrath. She wanted desperately go into the bathroom and take another bath or a shower. She stayed in her room feeling humiliated and dirty. Kim thought as she lay there of how she wanted to crawl up under a rock to die.

"The girl has been through enough. Please let her alone. She doesn't need to hear your mouth, especially when you're drunk!" George pleaded although it didn't stop Joyce from chastising Kim verbally. She continued to humiliate her for hours.

Kim was grateful, however, in the fact that George now stood up for her immensely. He had never taken her side before this day. She felt somewhat loved. She heard the telephone ring and could tell from George's tone that it was the police. George was once again saying blissful things about her.

"Sure, you can talk to her. Come on over," George told the authorities.

When the police arrived, George knocked on the door and insisted that Kim come out of her bedroom to talk to them. "I don't want to talk about it anymore!"

Kim felt as if it were happening all over again, especially when she talked about her unfortunate situation.

"If she refuses to talk with us then there is nothing we can do to help her," one officer said.

"Come on out here!" George commanded. "These police officers are here to help you. It's not your fault what happened. So, please come on out here. Don't let me have to take this door down!"

Knowing that George would keep to his word and do exactly that, she came out of the room. She sat down and the police began to ask her all the questions that she didn't want to answer.

"Do you know the man's name that attacked you? How did you get to his house? Had you been over there before?

"No, I had never met him before that night. He drove me to his house.

"Therefore he didn't force you to get into the car, nor to go with him home. You went with him willingly. What were you wearing? Did you go to the hospital?" He asked her question after question, barely giving her the opportunity to answer them.

These were all the questions that Kim didn't want to answer but she did. She answered all the horrible questions and while her parents sat listening to each answer. Joyce's face showed continuous disbelief as she shook her head in disbelief. The police seemed as disgusted with Jason as Kim was as she answered their questions.

"Thanks very much Kim. You have been very cooperative. We will call you as soon as we have him in custody," the officer said. They shook George's hand on the way out of the house. "We'll need you to bring them down town to identify him," he continued.

Kim went back into her room with Felicia. Somehow, she seemed to appreciate the fact of being able to hide behind a locked door, especially now that Felicia was no longer a bother.

"Telephone Kim," George yelled.

She opened the door and went into her father's bedroom where the telephone sat behind his lazy-boy chair on his chest stand.

"Nichol, Jason's sister, told us that the police came to pick him up for questioning last week. He came home today," Jessica told.

"What happened? What do you mean he's home? Jason's in jail, isn't he? Nichol was asking Genie many questions about what happened that night. Genie didn't tell her anything. His sister acted like she didn't believe that Jason had raped me."

"I don't feel like talking Jessica. I'll call you back later," Kim promised.

Joyce had gotten drunker and was still walking around the house crying and acting crazy.

"It's your fault! It's all your fault, Kim. If you had been in the house, this would have never happened. You brought it upon yourself. You need to cry! Cry... you stupid whore!"

Kim ran rapidly into the room and locked the door. She could hear her parents in their room talking about what had happened to her.

"You know it's not Kim's fault that she was raped. You shouldn't have said those horrible things to her!"

"She's to blame for what happened! It wouldn't have happened if she had stayed home! She never listens!"

"That doesn't make it her fault. I wished I knew where he lived... it's his fault. I would go over there and kill him!"

"He probably didn't rape her at all. If he did rape her, then I'm certain Jessica and her sisters had their hands in it. They planned the entire situation! I've told my girls about being trustworthy. Friends... they always have to have their friends. I never had friends and that is exactly the reason why. You just cannot trust anyone these days. Those Barbers'... I told Kim they were going to get her in a lot of trouble!" Joyce was drunk and babbling on as usual.

These thoughts of Jessica's betrayal went on in Kim's head as she lay there in her room. In her depression she began to think that maybe Joyce had a point. Perhaps Jessica could have been behind her attack and her humiliation. As she lay there she began to feel guilty about thinking negative thoughts about her dear friend. *Maybe she had a lot of soul searching to do within herself*, she thought.

Chapter 13

Kim stayed in her room for three days becoming lost in self-pity. She didn't see or hear Felicia. Nor did she hear her mother yelling and screaming at her. She got lost within her own personal prayers.

"Speak Lord. Tell me what I did that was so bad that you would allow this to happen to me. Please Lord... let me see a sign if Jessica had anything to do with this cruel thing."

Three days past and Kim still had no answers to why this had happened to her. On the forth day it was time for her and her parents to go down to the precinct to talk to the Chief of Police. Time for her to go press rape charges against Jason. Kim's parents were there during her questioning.

This made it hard for her to answer in detail what had happened to her — once again. She felt dirty and embarrassed talking about it in front of her parents.

"Can my parents leave the room while I answer your questions?"

"Since you are fifteen years old one of your parents will have to remain in the room. It's the law."

Again Kim explained in gory details... her rape. She sat there feeling dirty, used and melancholic inside. She felt as if she had been raped once again. Afterwards they went home. Kim was too embarrassed to go back to school and even to walk down the street to the corner store.

Kim's boyfriend from school, Joshua, kept calling and calling. Joshua was very handsome. He was about 5'9 and a varsity football player. All the girls at school wanted to date him and Kim was extremely lucky to have him. She couldn't find the words to talk to him. How could she possibly tell him what had happened to her? She couldn't, she just couldn't tell him. Finally, Kim accepted his call.

"Telephone, Kim," George said.

Kim knew that it was Joshua calling.

"Hey, how are you," Kim said, that afternoon. "I don't feel like taking."

"What's wrong with you Kim? Why haven't you been to school?"

"I haven't been feeling well, Joshua. You know, I don't think that I want to see you anymore." She hung up the telephone quickly. Joshua didn't call back.

When they arrived to court Kim and her parents went in the courtroom and sat quietly.

"Is he here?" Joyce whispered.

"There he is," George said pointing him out to Joyce. Kim was astonished and marvel how George knew what Jason looked like.

Jason sat adjacent of them, with that ugly smirk on his Face where he appears relaxed.

"*I should have stabbed him with that knife when I had the chance,*" she thought.

Kim stared him in his face and couldn't wait for the trial to begin. She was certain that she would see him cry out in pain as the sheriffs put him in handcuffs.

"George, you and your family follow me," a deputy said. Kim and her parent followed the deputy down a long narrow hallway where they got on an elevator. They arrived on the second floor where they entered into a small room. Kim's attorney, Mr. Dobbin sat at a round table across from Jason's attorney and another deputy.

"Are you sure that you will be able to go through with the questioning?" Kim's attorney asked her. "There are a lot of people here in the courtroom today."

"Yes, I'm sure that she will be able to go through with it," George insisted.

Kim shook her head in agreement with her father. "I don't think that it would be wise to have her get on the stand," Jason's attorney said. "She's so young and she will be under a lot of pressure out there. This is a small town... it will be in the newspapers. Everyone will read about it, even the people at her school. She wouldn't be able to hold her head up in town."

Jason's attorney made excuse after excuse as to why Kim should not testify.

"I'm not afraid! I want to go through with this. That is what we are here for isn't it."

"Since she's under age we'll leave it up to you."

Kim looked at her parents with plea in her eyes. However, without even looking at her George replied, "I guess you're right. It is very crowded in the courtroom. Maybe we could reschedule it for another day when it's less crowed."

"I don't think that is the answer. The courtroom is filled to capacity daily with so much crime going on now a day. It's almost always this crowded, if not more so," Mr. Dobbin continued.

"I guess we'll drop the charges," George said.

"No, you can't do this to me! I want to get him for what he did to me! He cannot just get away with this!"

131

"I said that we are going to just drop it and that's final!"

George insisted. Silence came over Kim as she looked directly in George's face.

"I hate you! I hate you! How can you do this to me?"

Kim returned to the courtroom where she turned and looked at Jason as he lay back on the bench with an arrogant look upon his face. He leaned forward as if to taunt her with a threat.

Kim ran out of the courthouse and out to the courtyard where she stood waiting for her parents. She smoked a cigarette as she stood there not caring if George saw her smoking or not. She could have cared less what he or anyone else thought of her at that moment. A joint would have been even better but Kim didn't have one. She was furious with Jason, her parents and the attorneys. Moreover... she was mad at herself.

How could they have done this to her — bringing her down to the courtroom and then dropping the charges? How could they drop the charges after she had humiliated herself by revamping the dreadful gory story in detail? she thought.

Discussing the details and undressing herself over again and in the presence of her parents only to have them just drop the charges against him.

"How could they do this to me?" she thought. *"Bring me*

132

here to look at his face, as he sat there, so unconcerned. To have me sit and look him in his face again and he looks in mine. Once again, successfully he take yet another part of me — my dignity!"

He had won and they had not even put up a fight. Kim felt terrible as she stood wondering how her parents could have made such a drastic decision concerning her rape trial. She had given them all or her trust, thinking that they would handle the trial as she would have. However, they had allowed him to attack her once again and in their presence. She wished that she were an adult and not the minor child whom stood with them that day.

"It didn't happen to them but to me! Jason stained my body with his mischief," she thought.

She had already been embarrassed enough and nothing could have embarrassed or hurt her more than Jason had already done.

"Why can't they understand?" she asked aloud.

She cried hysterically as she watched her parents come out of the courthouse. She didn't care who saw her talking to herself that afternoon. Standing there wondering why her lawyer and even Jason's lawyer couldn't see that she was strong enough to go to trial.

133

"Come on Kim, let's go," Joyce said. Kim didn't say a word as they walked slowly towards her but she continued pacing in the courtyard.

As they neared her, Kim turned her head to look the other way. She couldn't tolerate making eye contact with her hideous parents. She didn't want to get in the same car with them but she had no place to go. Kim walked slothfully behind them. With her head hung down, she got into the car.

"I better not see you around," Jason mumbled. "I'm going to kill you."

As Kim read his lips, she realized that Jason threatened to harm her. She eyed him as he stood in front of the courtyard and even as they drove away. She eyed him until she could see him no more.

"He is threatening me!" Kim told George.

"The police will be keeping a close eye on him after what he has done. Jason won't be pestering you or anyone else in Rocking Barrel for sometime."

Kim was still quite distraught with her parents that following day. She didn't want to stay around the house to look at them and she wanted to get out of there. She decided to return to school that morning. With her head hung down she walked to the bus stop. She noticed Jason's car parked adjacent to the bus stop when she held her head high. Petrified by his presence she stopped in her tracks. The bus was arriving and the children had begun to load the bus. She ran rapidly to the bus and took a seat hoping that Jason had not noticed her. She made no effort to look towards him once seated on the bus however she was quite aware of his presence.

"Jason was parked in front of the bus stop," Kim whispered to her father over the telephone. She called him immediately after arriving to school.

"Who was parked in front of the bus stop?"

"Jason was parked there!"

"Calm down... it is going to be okay. I'll call the police and we'll keep an eye out for him."

Kim could hardly concentrate in school knowing that there was a possibility that he would also be sitting there when she returned home. Nervous and concerned, Kim kept quiet. There was no way she could confide her fear to anyone at school without telling them that she had been raped. She didn't want to tell a soul.

At the end of school, the bell finally rang as Kim sat nervously in a daze contemplating whether or not she should stay at school or go home.

"Hurry up Kim before we miss the bus," Michelle, her neighbor, warned.

"I'm coming," Kim said as she ran out of the door behind her. The bus was just about to leave.

George was standing at the bus stop when Kim returned home. She was quite relieved and felt safe when she saw him there. She turned to see if Jason was lurking somewhere in the vicinity and sure his car approaching slowly towards her. George saw him too but never said a word. He held Kim's hand tightly pulling her closer towards him as they walked briskly down the street and into the house. Once inside George called the police. Kim continued to stand at the door watching Jason as he drove his car up to the front of her house where he parked. She stood there looking him directly in his eyes not showing any fear. As George now approached, the door behind her, Jason drove slowly away from the house.

"I was hoping that he would have continued to sit there until the police arrived. I dare he park his car in front of my house like that — just, who in the HELL does he think he is!"

"The police should be here any minute now. I sure hope that he comes back around when they get here."

"What's going on George?" the officer asked.

136

"We recently filed a rape charge against Jason Smith and he has since been harassing my daughter. He parked across the street this morning and watched her as she left out for school. A minute ago, he parked in front of the house. That's when I called you guys."

"I got his information and we are going to go over to his house to pay him a little visit."

"Do I have to go down and take out a restraining order on him?"

"No, you won't have to worry about him coming around harassing you or your daughter again," the officer promised. These were words that Kim had heard before and hoped never to hear again.

Chapter 14

Months went by and Jason had not come around. Nonetheless Kim refused to leave the house alone in fear of him. She would wait for Nicholas or Borne to go with her to the park because she refused to venture out on her own.

One afternoon when she was at the park with Jessica, she noticed Jason's car parked across the street. She had felt that someone was watching her. Such as she did the morning Jason watched her at the bus stop. He sat in his car smoking a cigarette while watching her.

"Nicholas, Nicholas!" she yelled frantically taking his attention from off of the basket ball game.

"What?"

"There's Jason. He's following me again!" she said. She began to cry hysterically and ran over to Nicholas.

"Come on Otis," Nicholas urged. They ran towards Jason's car as he accelerated his gas pedal and drove away wildly.

"Gosh I wish I could have gotten my hands on him," Otis, Nicholas's best friend, said in disappointment.

Kim knew from the expression on his face and the tension in his voice that Otis knew what Jason had done to her. Otis and

Nicholas had been the best of friends since she could remember. He had a huge crush on Jessica and wanted desperately to give her the world. Unfortunately she didn't find him at all appealing.

"You and Otis would make a good couple Jessica. Don't you think that he is really handsome?"

"He's too young for me and you know he doesn't have any money. Maybe I'll think about it when he gets older — and some money."

Weeks following this conversation Tessa, Kim's schoolmate, moved into the house directly across the street from Jessica.

"Kim, do you know that guy sitting over there on that porch?" she asked. She pointed her finger across the street at Jessica's house. Kim looked over and Otis and Mr. Barber sat out on the porch.

"That's Otis, Nicholas's best friend. Isn't he fine?"

"Is he ever?" Tessa confirmed. She fell in love with him at first sight, unlike Jessica.

"You can forget about him Tessa. He only has eyes for Jessica. He has been trying to get with her for years," she explained.

"Jessica was one of the first people that I met when I

moved over here. Why have I not seen the two of them together?

"That would be something, seeing the two of them together," Kim said jokingly. "I thought that he was her brother, cousin or uncle. Especially since, he is always sitting on the porch with her father. I should have known as handsome as he looks that he was not available. Other than speaking to me, he barely even looks my way. So, how long have they been dating?"

"Dating... they're not dating. Jessica wouldn't be caught dead with him. She thinks he is too young for her."

"What's funny? She must be crazy not to talk to him, I would die to go on a date with him."

When Kim returned home, later that afternoon, Otis was visiting Nicholas.

"Otis, guess who likes you?"

"Who, Jessica?" he replied excitedly.

"No, Tessa."

"Who's Tessa?"

"She's the new girl who just moved across the street from Jessica."

"Oh, she's cute." He said now showing a huge grin upon his face.

Remarkably weeks later to Kim's surprise, Tessa informed

her that she and Otis had begun to date. Since she hadn't been over to Jessica or Tessa's house in a while, the news came as such a shock. The following weekend Kim walked with Nicholas to Tessa's house. When she arrived there, she was abruptly side tracked by Jessica who was calling her across the street to her porch.

"I can't believe that you are going over to her house! You are supposed to be my friend! You walk right pass my house and not say a word to me!"

"Hello Jessica, how are you? Kim said sarcastically.

"Oh, now you say hello. What are you doing hanging with Tessa?"

"Tessa and I have been friends for a while."

"I don't think you should be hanging with her!"

"Jessica, you can't tell me who to hang with. You don't have that right!"

"So I hear that she is dating Otis. What is up with that? I mean she didn't even know him except for the fact that she saw him coming over here to visit me. Now she's dating him, Jessica said furiously. She makes me sick. What kind of friend are you? How can you be so cant by hanging out with her?"

"I am not getting in the middle of you and Tessa's quarrel,

Jessica. I still consider myself your friend. Honestly, why is it now that Tessa is dating Otis that you find this to be such a problem? Remember, you said that you were not interested in him. Unexpectedly, you seem to be so concerned about who he is seeing. You appeared to be only using him when he wanted to be with you accepting what little money he had. Now that Tessa really cares for him, you're jealous."

"You need to mind your own business, Kim! Secondly, I don't believe that Otis's or my relationship should be of any concern to you. I think that it would be best for the two of us if you and I just ended our friendship today.

"I agree with you totally," Kim said turning her back towards Jessica and walking away. She returned to Tessa's house leaving Jessica standing alone on her porch. Despite Jessica's ill weathered feelings, Tessa and Otis continued to date. Kim continued to spend time at Tessa's house.

"I don't know why it is every time that Otis comes to visit me Jessica summons him over to her house," Tessa confided to Kim that afternoon. "I am so frustrated with her trying to come between us. I asked Otis to stop going over there. Every time she yells for him to come over he still goes running to her beckon call."

"What did he say?"

"He had the audacity to tell me that he and Jessica have been friends far longer than the two of us have been dating."

"What he said, is true, Tessa. You can't expect for him to just come over here and ignore her."

"Yes I do expect him to just ignore her," Tessa, said. "I mean... I like him a lot and I know that I am the new one in the neighborhood. I don't want to cause any confusion but she can't keep trying to come between us like this. Otis has obviously made his decision as to whom he wants. She really should back up off of him."

"Just ignore Jessica. Otis is a faithful guy. I'm sure that they don't be talking about anything when he does go over there," Kim advised.

Jessica remained furious with Kim for months. Even though Kim spoke to her, Jessica never bothered to reply. Kim was not sure why but deep inside she was glad that the two of them were not speaking.

Maybe deep inside of her, she too blamed Jessica for Jason's attacking her. She felt that she could have somehow stopped her from getting into the car with Jason, instead of encouraging her to do so. Perhaps it was because she felt betrayed by the fact that Jessica refused to come to court to be a witness. Her excuse being that she didn't witness the actual rape.

Kim felt that Jessica could have verified the only reason why she had agreed to get in the car with Jason was that he had promised to take her home. If she had only come to court to explain how bad she looked that morning when she showed up at her doorstep. If she had only put forth an effort, Kim could have understood her friend. However, she now had no confidence or trust in Jessica.

A year past and Kim thought Jason to be out of her life. Spontaneously, he began to appear at different places she would go. Kim was once again afraid for her life.

"Kim, my cousin Jaquan called and asked me to telephone you to see if you would like to go out with him sometime," Tessa informed.

Kim was delighted that Jaquan was interested in dating her and thinking fast she said, "I would love to go out with him!"

Along with meeting Jaquan at Tessa's house, Kim had seen him around town many times before. She knew this, because everyone in town was afraid of him and she hoped that Jason would be too. Jaquan had a considerable reputation of being a ruthless, heartless and devious man. He was an older man, 25 years old and stood 6'2 — taller than Jason. His weight was well over 195 pounds. Kim felt that Jason wouldn't dare follow her around once he saw or heard that she and Jaquan was a couple.

"Jaquan just pulled up in front of the house Kim.

We're going to go to the park. Do you want to come with us?"

"Sure, come by to pick me up," Kim said.

"Be ready, because we will be there in about fifteen minutes."

"Okay."

Jaquan sat out in his pick up truck while Tessa came in to get Kim. When Kim got in the truck they went to a liquor house. Most teenagers hung out there because they allowed them to drink. After entering the house Jaquan sat at a card table. He watched Kim as she sat nervously across the room. She looked in his big brown eyes and they appeared warm and sincere. She knew he wanted her as much as she needed him.

Feeling safe and content in his presence she walked over to him and gave him a shy kiss on his cheek. She then returned to the room where she had been sitting nervously.

"I want you," she lipped to Jaquan.

145

He smiled shyly and continued to eye her above his hand. His smile remained sly and sexy.

"Come with me Kim," Tessa said.

"I forgot to tell you that Jaquan's ex-girlfriend comes here sometimes. She is very jealous of him," Tessa told.

"Thanks for the heads up," Kim said.

Although she was not at all concerned about Jaquan's ex-gir she needed his protection. No one was going to stop her from getting it.

"Is that her?" Kim asked Tessa. She noticed a woman standing close to Jaquan.

"Tessa shook her head in agreement."

"What are you doing here? I thought you weren't feeling good," Kim over heard her say.

"I told you I would be over there later," he whispered in a demanding low tone. He grabbed her by the arm and shoved her back out the front door. Kim noticed this as she watched his every move from across the room. Jaquan remained outside talking to this woman for fifteen minutes. When he came back into the house, he stood beside Kim.

"I'll be right back to take you home," he whispered in her ear. "Don't go anywhere."

"Okay, I want."

Jaquan walked back out the door and he stayed gone for quite a while before returning to Kim.

"I'm ready to go," she told him when he returned.

"Where's Tessa?"

"She's in there," Kim said pointing towards the room where he had played cards.

Jaquan went and got her and they left. He dropped

Tessa off at home first. Kim appreciated that because she wanted to spend time alone with him. "Is it possible for us to see each other again?" "Sure. I don't see why not," Kim replied flirtatiously. "So can I get your telephone number?

"Yes." She wrote her telephone number down on a piece of paper and handed it to him. She kissed him on his cheek.

"Come here," he said. He pulled her close to him and kissed her on her mouth. "I'll see you later," he said

Kim walked towards the house as he watched her patiently. Kim had thoughts of only Jaquan that night. He called her the following afternoon when she returned home from school.

"Can I come get you?"

"Sure, bring Tessa with you."

She wanted to keep the fact that she was seeing him a secret from her family.

"I'll pick her up before coming to get you," he replied.

Kim and Jaquan saw each other heavily for about a month. This was before anyone in her family knew that she was seeing him. Otis was the first to find out about the two. He saw her kissing him passionately one evening as they sat parked in his truck in front of Tessa's house. He walked up to the truck and tapped lightly on Jaquan's window.

"Kim Nicholas was looking for you earlier," he said.

"Okay... thank you," she said.

That night when she returned home, she found that Nicholas waiting up for her that evening.

"What were you doing in the truck with Jaquan?"

"What are you talking about?" Kim tried to deny the fact that she was seeing Jaquan.

"Otis told me that he saw you kissing him in his truck."

Kim's insight warned her that Otis would tell Nicholas about her and Jaquan's special moment.

"You and Otis need to mind your business."

She walked out of the kitchen as the telephone began to ring. To her astonishment, it was Jaquan.

"Hey, Jaquan."

"Can you come out?"

"No now is not a good time for me."

"Okay then I'll call you back some other time."

"That would be better," Kim said. She hung up the telephone.

"Kim, who is that man who keeps calling here for you?" George asked. "He sounds much older than you."

"That's someone who goes to my school," Kim ensured.

She didn't call Jaquan back that night however she went to Tessa's home the following afternoon and called him.

"Jaquan you have to stop calling me so much. My father's asking me questions about you. He knows that you are older... he could tell by your voice," she explained.

"I don't care Kim. Why are you trying to hide us from everyone? I thought you cared for me."

"I don't know."

"I'm on my way to get you."

"I'm not home Jaquan."

"Where are you?"

"I'm over Tessa's house."

"Well, I'll come get you from there."

"Okay, she told him."

Kim went out to the truck when he pulled up. "Where are we going?"

"I'm taking you home. I think it's about time that I met your parents."

"No, you can't do that."

"I can and I am."

He drove towards Kim's house. When they arrived there, Jaquan got out of the truck and walked around to open her door. He held her by the hand as they walked towards the house. As they entered the living room, Joyce came out of the kitchen.

"Oh, Kim, it's you. Who is that nice looking gentleman you have with you?"

"Mom, this is Jaquan."

"Hi how are you?" Jaquan said with his deep voice. The thickness of his tone brought George out of his bedroom.

"Hi how are you doing? I'm George, Kim's father."

"Hello Sir, I'm doing just fine. I'm Jaquan a close friend of Kim... it's good to finally meet you."

"It's good to meet you," George said.

He shook Jaquan's hand and returned to his bedroom. Kim was surprised that he had come out of his room to meet Jaquan. She and Jaquan sat out on the front porch where he continued to hold her hand.

"Were you holding it when my father came out?"

"Holding what... your hand? I'm sure I was. Why, I know you're not shy Kim."

"No... not really. I was just wondering if he had seen you holding my hand."

Jaquan smiled and kissed her gently on her cheek, causing her to be even more nervous. Wooing her with his visit to her home, Kim continued to date him. They began going out to supper. She even went to his basketball games where she sat out on the front row. Soon, everyone in Rocking Barrel knew that the two were an item. Although Kim was quite content with Jaquan, many of her classmates teased her because of his age.

"Where's your daddy? Kim... girl you know you shouldn't be seeing Jaquan. He is too old for you... you can do better and besides he's crazy. Have you lost your mind." Her classmates as well as Nicholas taunted her repeatedly regarding their relationship.

Kim never responded to the ill responses that she received

from the boys at her school or Nicholas. As usual she only walked away quietly. She refused to listen to anything negative that anyone had to say concerning Jaquan. He was the only person who had succeeded in keeping Jason away from taunting her. As she began to get comfortable with Jaquan and their relationship, he brought up the conversation of her not wanting to be alone with him.

"Why don't you ever like being alone with me?" Jaquan asked of her.

"Don't be silly Jaquan. We always spend time alone."

"Yes I guess we do... at games or when we go out to eat — never alone. Whenever I ask you to go somewhere secluded so that we can be alone... you always say no."

"When have I told you no?"

"The time I asked you to come to my house and the time I asked you to let's get a room," he refreshed her memory. "I don't think that you want to be alone with me," he said.

Kim hoped the conversation would not come up, especially, not so soon. She wanted his friendship and his protection. She had some how forgotten about his feelings. She hadn't imagined the two of them making love. They were having so much fun and he appeared so content with just being with her.

Jaquan was kissing her all over her body while taking off her clothes. Although she wanted desperately to say stop... she couldn't. She knew that Jaquan was deserving of her love. She pushed him gently away but Jaquan continued to kiss her passionately. His lips, soft and tender. She liked his touch as well as his kisses. Her body began to stiffen up on her and him.

"What's wrong Kim? Why are you just lying there?

"Like what?"

"You act like you're afraid."

"Afraid. Why do you say that?"

"Why are you so stiff and not moving? I'm not going to hurt you."

"I know you're not going to hurt me Jaquan. I don't know... I guess I'm not in the mood. I love you. Come here," Jaquan said.

He held her tightly... but gently in his arms. He could feel her fear and coldness. Kim began to cry and the tears flowed swiftly down onto her face.

"Please stop crying Kim. Why are you so afraid? Is it me? Is it something I did?" Jaquan continued to hold her in his arms rocking her gently back and forth. Although still crying Kim felt peaceful in his arms. "What is it Kim? Tell me what's on your mind. You can talk to me about anything. I know that you heard

153

about what happened to me in college. Is that what's scaring you? I didn't mean to do it but I did. It was her fought not mines."

"What are you talking about? What happened when you were in college?" Kim asked pushing him forcefully away. She wondered what Jaquan was now referring to and thought that he too had raped a woman. Aware now that Kim knew nothing about what had happened to him in college, he evaded her question.

"Are you acting this way because you were raped? Tessa told me you had been raped and that some guy had been following you.

"She told you. Why would she tell you about that? How could she betray me like this?"

"She didn't tell me the entire story... she was just worried about you," he continued in her defense.

"Yes, I was raped by this guy named Jason Smith."

"He's the one who raped you. I went to high school with that creep. He was a creep then and I see that he is still a creep. I'll kill him!" he said with promise as he pulled her gently back into his arms.

"So don't evade the question. What were you trying to tell me about you and college?"

"Do you know Gina Smalls?"

"No, I don't. Who is she?"

"Gina was the only girl whom I knew when I arrived to college. She was a cheerleader, from Rocking Barrel. One night after our game the two of us got together at the victory party. We were both drunk that night and she asked if she could come back with me to my apartment. This was my senior year and with my scholarship funds, I could afford to live off campus. Gina began to undress as soon as I closed the door. We made love.

Before I knew it... she was giving me head. She asked me to go down on her and I agreed. We were in the sixty-nine position when she entered her tongue into my butt. I got so excited that I inadvertently made a bowel movement on her."

"You did what? It's not funny and you shouldn't be laughing. That is nasty! How in the world did that happen?"

"I know it's not funny. I might be laughing now but I surely wasn't laughing then. I don't know how it happened. I've never had anyone give me head. I guess I got too excited. She, however, thought that I had done it purposely. She put her clothes on and ran out the door. Minutes later, the police were knocking on my door."

"What? What happened then?

"She told the police what had happened but she said that I

had purposely made the bowel movement on her face."

"So what happened next?"

"I was arrested for an indecent liberty. There was a write up about it in the local newspaper, as well as in our school paper. I was kicked off of the basketball team and expelled from college."

"I'm sorry to hear that. I know that it was embarrassing for you and your parents."

Jaquan and Kim made passionate love that night. He asked her to give him head but of course, there was no way that she would. Especially after him, telling her what happened to Gina. His persistent agitated her, so that she immediately began to get dressed.

"Please take me home Jaquan. I've gotten a headache now with all this talk about Jason and Gina. I can't believe that you would have the audacity to ask me to perform this same action on you."

"I'm sorry Kim. I didn't mean to upset you."

"Just please take me home."

"Sure, no problem, come on. Let's go," he said leading her out the door. The ride home was very quiet.

"Good night Jaquan I will call you tomorrow," she said having arrived home. Kim however didn't call him the following day and she didn't call him for several weeks.

"Jaquan really wants to see you Kim. He is always talking about you and he really misses you." Tessa telephoned to say.

"I don't want to see him anymore."

"Why don't you want to see him anymore? He broke up with his girlfriend for you, Kim. You know he loves you."

"I know he loves me Tessa but I don't love him. I don't think that I ever will. I don't think I know what love is anymore."

"Hold on Kim." Tessa said.

"Hi Kim, I miss you baby. Please let me come get you."

Tessa had given Jaquan the telephone and he tried to smooth the air with Kim.

"I need to see you. Do you want to go to the park? Please say yes. It's been too long since I've seen you."

"Sure, come pick me up in an hour. I have to get dressed." Tessa had broken it off with Otis, of course because of Jessica and was now seeing one of Jaquan's friends. He and Jaquan sat out in the truck as Tessa came in to get Kim.

"Jaquan was so happy that you agreed to come with us. Girl he really loves you. I have never seen him act this way about any one."

Jaquan was really gentle and sweet at the park as always with Kim. This was contradictory to all the bad rumors that Kim had heard about him around town. When they arrived to the park, he held her hand as she got out of the truck. He even pushed her on the swing.

"We need to talk, let's walk down near the tennis courts," he whispered.

There was no one playing tennis that day, as well as other days, which made it the perfect place for them to talk.

"Why have you been avoiding me?"

"I don't know. I'm just so confused. I thought I was ready for us but I realized the other night when we were together that I'm not. As much as I would love to lay with you, I couldn't."

"I care for you a lot Jaquan. I'm just not ready for a relationship as if you need and deserve. I think it would be better for the both of us, if we didn't see each other anymore. Things are going too fast for me. I'm not ready yet."

"Are you still confused because of what Jason did to you? I would never hurt you Kim."

"That has a lot to do with it. I'm just all confused inside right now. I don't think a relationship would be the best thing for me."

158

"I understand... I just needed to talk to you to make sure that it wasn't anything that I had said or done."

"No, it's not you at all Jaquan. It's me and I guess bad timing."

"Do you think we can remain friends?"

"Yes, of course. Are you ready to go? Yes, let's go."

He gave her a passionate kiss and grabbed her hand as they walked back to the bench where Tessa and Junior sat talking. Kim returned home where she went into her room. She just wanted to get some rest. All that talk about Jason had depressed her. Usually when she spent time with Jaquan, Jason was never on her mind. She hadn't seen him at all since the word got out that she and Jaquan were dating. Rumor around Rocking Barrel was that Jaquan had murdered him but Kim didn't think that to be true.

Kim was a junior in high school now and wanted to get her mind back into her schoolbooks. She knew that once she graduated that she could move far away from Jason and Felicia. Although she would miss Jaquan, she knew that it would never work with their age difference.

Chapter 15

Felicia was getting much worse.

"Daddy, can I sleep out in the living room on the sofa? I don't want to sleep in there with Felicia... she's crazy!"

"Suit yourself," George said.

Kim brought her pillow and blanket out into the living room. Sleeping on the sofa went well for about two nights. Felicia too began bringing her pillow and sheet to sleep on the sofa next Kim.

She began making an appearance every night when she would talk to her invisible friends and laugh aloud to herself. This was a tremendous annoyance to Kim. Becoming exasperated by Felicia's presence, she stormed down the corridor. She knocked on George's bedroom door seeking his assistance.

"Daddy, please make Felicia go to bed. I've got to get some sleep, because I have to go to school in the morning."

I really would like to get some sleep. Please, make her go back into her bedroom!"

Her parent's didn't respond to her cry for help.

"Mommy — mommy, please open the door," she pleaded.

Although there was no response to her plea, she didn't give up. She stood at the door waiting for a response.

She felt pushed against a cement wall with nowhere to run as the walls appear to be closing in on her. There was no place for Kim to go. Her parents lay in their bedroom with deaf ears as they pretend not to hear her knocking. She sat on the floor crying hysterically and feeling abandoned. Once again Kim lies there on the floor as she cries herself to sleep. Joyce finally came out of her room, that following morning.

"Why didn't you open the door?"

"Open the door for what?"

"Didn't you hear me banging on your door?"

"No, I didn't. Why were you banging on my door?"

"Felicia... she walked and talked all night. I didn't get any sleep. I'm not going to school today!"

"I don't know what is going on with you two but you're going to have to just ignore Felicia."

"That's easier said than done. You, daddy, Borne and even Nicholas can ignore her — locked away in your rooms! I don't have any room or door to lock. Remember I sleep out in the living room."

Although Kim expressed her concern that morning, there were no changes made to aide her or her concerns. She continued knocking on her parents' bedroom door, nightly. She even knocked on Borne and Nicholas's door.

Night after night she knocked but got no help. She just cries herself to sleep.

Sleeping out in the living room was far better for her than sleeping in that locked bedroom with Felicia. She felt more protected there and didn't fear Felicia stabbing her in her sleep. This was what she continuously threatened to do to Kim. Kim often wondered how her family would feel if they were to find her all cut up into little tiny pieces... in the morning. She felt that maybe this would be the only way that she would be taken seriously. Only then would Felicia get the mental help that she so needed.

Albeit Felicia came out in the living room daily to sit out with her Kim pretended not to see her there. She knew that it was not her place to scorn her about sitting in the living room. Therefore she never said a word. However she would just watch television. Moreover... it was indeed the family room. She wouldn't sit long but long enough to aggravate Kim. Then she would go back into her bedroom locking the door behind her. This aggravated Kim even more because she had nowhere to go to be alone.

With all her pleading for help her family seemed uncaring of her fears. Borne and Nicholas often laughed Felicia way. They didn't want to think about it, so they often joked with Kim about Felicia's illness. No one, other than Kim, took Felicia's illness serious in the Tucker's home. The torture Kim endured with Felicia was a continuous chipping away of her being and peace of mind. Her threat to murder her in her sleep was certainly no joking matter. Now and in her own paranoia state, Kim too felt that she was going insane. She strongly felt that her entire family was in on the plan along with Felicia to kill her.

"How could they just lay there, night after night in their warm beds? While she lay fearful for her life, they remain locked away behind closed doors. Were they not aware or just uncaring of her safety, she thought. *How could they leave her alone with her?"*

It was obvious that Felicia was pure evil and cruel. Felicia continuously pursued her. Now she began to lie there across from Kim watching, whispering and laughing. Kim felt much like a victim in her own home. She considered if indeed she could still call this her home since she felt more like a border than a family member.

She no longer had sympathy for Felicia or her illness. Now she had become so frustrated with her that she wanted her gone. She wanted Felicia out of her life and by any means necessary.

Kim began to plan her own strategy to protect herself from Felicia. She too began sleeping with a knife underneath her pillow.

"How could she possibly find it in her heart to have sympathy for someone that she now felt to be holding her hostage?"

Kim had nothing but total hatred in her heart towards Felicia and now she was losing trust in the rest of her family. No longer did she run and hide from Jason but she now also ran to protect her sanity. Realizing that this feeling of day-to-day terror and torment was not healthy she wanted someone to turn to for help. Although she longed for someone to talk too — there was no one. She buried her feelings deep inside and hoped that eventually her problems would resolve on there own.

Fall came and Kim began to go out with her classmates and anyone else who would let her hangout with them. Oftentimes she would spend the night with Tessa and Jessica. Sometimes she would stay out with strange guys whom she knew nothing about... or did she care to know them. She only met them along the way home and would spend the night with them. She refused to go home and would do anything to get a good night sleep. She even began to pick up older men. She didn't care as long as she didn't have to go home to deal with Felicia. Of course her parents were disturbed that she was staying out and sometimes two to three nights a week. Uncaring to her parent's opinion — as they were in giving no assistance to her regarding Felicia's vengeance. She felt safer in the street than she did in her own home. Therefore she continued to hangout.

"I'm going to have you put in a girl's home if you continue this disobedience!" George said.

"I don't care what you do. Anything is better than staying in that room with Felicia."

"You're just using Felicia as your escape goat. She really is not that bad. She doesn't seem to bother me and your mother or anyone else in the house."

"Why don't you try sleeping in the room with her? You'll see how crazy she is, indubitably. I can't believe you don't hear her and the madness she speaks. She giggles and laughs all night. I'm not going to stay in that room with her any longer! I can't even sleep in the living room without her following me!"

"You'll sleep where I damn well tell you too in my house!" George concluded.

After this night Kim began to stay home more. George's threat of putting her in a girl's home seemed sincere this night. She went into her bedroom thinking maybe she would get a good night sleep. However the room reaped with a bad odor.

"What is that awful smell? It smells horrible in here. Felicia, why don't you go and take a bath or something."

"I smell like roses. Can't you smell me? I smell like sweet perfume," Felicia said.

She then sat there smoking her cigarettes. She sat laughing to herself. Although certain that Felicia's laughter not necessarily directed towards her undoubtedly Kim found it quite aggravating. From the appearance of Felicia Kim was certain that it was her scent, which filling the air. She had not been bathing, again.

Felicia would go into the bathroom daily as if to bathe however it was obvious she had not. She would come out smelling the same, if not worse, as she had before entering the bathroom. Kim imagined her standing in the dark running water and staring in the mirror. It was obvious that this is all she did there since her deadly dreadful scent still lingered. The bathroom too began to reap of her bodily odor that smelt like mildew and month old wet cigarette butts.

Felicia could be so embarrassing and especially when Kim had company. Albeit everyone in town was aware of her illness her behavior remained an embarrassment to Kim. Quite annoying to her when she would come out of her room and sit out on the sofa along beside her quest. She always sat at the corner of the sofa where she smoked cigarette after cigarette. One after the other — laughing or grinning to herself.

Kim found it hard to imagine anyone understanding Felicia's behavior. Although she tried desperately to ignore Felicia's presence her unruly disturbances would continue to haunt her. She would often invite her guest outside on the front porch to rid herself of Felicia's dreadful odor.

Felicia was still quite beautiful... especially when she got dressed in her fine clothes. Her face was pure-silky and naturally even-toned. She had the prettiest light-brown hair that draped down her shoulders and light-green eyes. Anyone could see how she became one of the top models in the Nation's Capital. She modeled at Macy's, Lord and Taylor's and Bloomindales.

Joyce some how found amusement in the fact that Felicia would get made-up every three months or so in her fine clothes. She would parade up and down the streets of Rocking Barrel. Kim, however, found it to be very annoying. Most of these clothes, she acquired back when she was modeling. She would stand in front of the mirror making her face and combing her hair for hours and as soon as the sun went down, she would walk down the street to the corner store where she would stay for hours.

"It's time for her three-month man search," Joyce would say jokingly and Kim imagined this to be true.

This was mainly because when Felicia did return home she was so much happier and seemed more satisfied. She would bring back beer and a couple of packs of cigarettes. She was getting a disability check in which she had transferred from Washington. No, one understood why she couldn't stretch the check out through the month, since she had no bills. She would only buy cigarettes and candy bars. George would take her to the dollar store every month to get any personal items she needed. Kim and Joyce were so happy when her check arrived, because Felicia would seem much happier. Especially since, she had her cigarettes.

Like an alarm clock, she would wait about five minutes before it was time for George to leave. She would begin slamming the kitchen cabinets. She did this mainly to piss him off before going to work, especially when he refused to buy her cigarettes.

She also wanted to intimidate Kim and Joyce into going into Joyce's bedroom in which they often did when she acted in this manner. George became furious with Felicia's behavior when one afternoon before his leaving for work, she came out of her room and began to throw glasses and everything else in her path like the Tasmanian devil.

"Felicia, what in the HELL is wrong with you? He said, running out of his room. Don't be breaking up my S H I T! I didn't buy these things in here for you to break!"

"Leave me the HELL alone! Just leave me alone. Do not let me do an exorcist on your ASS! Do you want to see me turn my head around... do you? You know you had better leave me alone before I throw you out of that window," she threatened. "I get tired of you coming in my room at night too and I am not your wife and don't you bother me anymore!"

"Girl, you really are crazy!" he said for the first time since Felicia returned to Rocking Barrel. Kim shook her head in agreement with him. "If you keep this up I am going to have you institutionalized."

This frightened Kim, the thought of her speaking on performing an exorcist. Kim knew that Felicia was not crazy, from the time that she arrived. Enduring the torture that Felicia caused her, for more than two years, Kim knew something possessed her. Some evil desolate spirit, maybe but in no way was she crazy.

Kim stood in amazement waiting anxiously for Felicia to turn her head around in a circle or to lift George up off the floor. She was certain that Felicia was possessed and had such powers. Felicia however used no powers this day. Instead, George lifted her up off the floor by her legs as she beat him violently on his back. He took her into her bedroom and threw her onto her bed. He then began to take the hinges off the bedroom door.

"You had better stay in this room and keep your mouth shut," he warned before grabbing his lunch bag and walking out the door.

"Joyce, you call me if you need for me to come home," he said on his way out of the door.

Felicia finally calmed down and went into her room. She sat quiet for the remainder of the day. The following day, however, she was back to being the Tasmanian devil that she was. George had returned home from work and she began to pace the floor. She walked madly and rapidly back and forth throughout the house. She was cursing uncontrollable and chanting something underneath her breath.

Chapter 16

Joyce and Kim could now depict the days when Felicia was going to act up. One of the first signs was her pacing back and forth. She would walk from the living room to Borne and Nicholas' room — they were never home. She would then walk back into the kitchen where she would slam the cabinet doors one by one. Afterwards she would stand at the bedroom door and watch them as they sat watching television.

"Felicia come in and sit down! Don't just stand there," Joyce often said.

She would never take Joyce up on her offer; however she would just stand speechless. Annoyingly she would laugh mischievously to herself and smoke cigarette after cigarette. She never said a word as she stood for hours. Never did she behave this way when George was at home… standing at Joyce's bedroom door.

When George was home, she would sit in her room quiet and innocently. However as soon as he would leave she would come stand at the door. Sometimes she would turn around in circles… cursing aloud or hold dialogue with herself. She often asked questions and answered them as well. Speaking forcefully she would give instructions as if speaking to a little child. It was hard to ignore her although Kim and Joyce did their best and sometimes she would even leave them alone.

George kept the hinges off Felicia's door for about a month before putting them back on her door. This delighted Kim since she could now hear when Felicia was coming out of her room. She felt a little more at ease knowing that she could put her guards up against Felicia. Yet nothing could prepare her for the day when she and Felicia got into a heated fight.

Felicia had come out of her room and stood at Joyce's bedroom door watching them as usual. This was a day when she would watch them for hours. Although they ignored her, she never budged. She refused to go away. Felicia had a soft and low voice but... the nastiest and craziest words would come out of it when she spoke. This day she just seemed to go on and on and with no ceasing.

"Damn the television! I'm the television," she insisted. You want to watch me... give me a cigarette!" she said. *She came and stood in front of the television set*.

"We don't have any cigarettes. Felicia go into the living room and leave us alone," Joyce instructed. "If you want to come in and watch television then please do so."

172

"I don't want to sit in here with you people. Just give me a cigarette!"

"For the last time Felicia I don't have any!"

Felicia turned and walked out of the room. Kim and Joyce heard her calling them bitches as she walked down the corridor. She ran up and down the corridor several times. The she ran back up the corridor and went into her bedroom where she remained silent for two-hours.

Just when Joyce and Kim felt relief — she came out of her room slamming the door forcefully behind her. She then ran frantically into the kitchen as if she was being chased. She began slamming the cabinet doors. Neither Joyce nor Kim knew what to say to calm her. They sat quietly in Joyce's bedroom looking at one another in awe.

Since she was being ignored... Felicia ran back into the living room like a wild animal. She was out of control. She picked up the sterling silver ashtray in which she had given Joyce one Christmas and threw it towards them. The ashtray missed Joyce's head by a little over an inch.

Kim considered what would have happened had the ashtray hit Joyce. Just the thought sent her into a rage and in her madness she jumped up out of the chair and hit Felicia in her

173

face. She hit her in the head several times and began to choke her. She too was out of control and unstoppable as she swung violently at Felicia. The frustration she had built up inside of her sent her into an uncontrollable rage and one she had never encountered.

"Stop hitting her Kim before you kill her!" Joyce yelled for her to stop.

Kim looked down at Felicia who lay powerlessly underneath her on the floor. As she continued to hold her forcefully down, she felt her weakening. Her face was red with wounds from the licks that Kim had bestowed upon her. Kim too weakened and as her strength weakened, Felicia's grew stronger. She almost tackled Kim down on the floor underneath her body with her strength.

"Let her go Kim," Joyce yelled.

"I'm not going to let her go... she's crazy!"

"Run in the room and I'll lock the door behind you."

"Okay but move out the way in case she throws something again."

Knowing that there would be no way for her to control Felicia once she let her go she hopped up and ran into Joyce's room. They locked the door behind her as Felicia was not far behind Kim.

"I'm going to get you bitches! You had better not come out of there!" Felicia warned as she banged on the door. "I'm going to kill you!" Her voice was dreadful and deep as she gave one final kick on the door. She then went back into her room and slammed it behind her. She stayed there for a while... screaming at the top of her lungs and throwing things against the wall.

Knowing no other way to get her under control Joyce called the police. When they finally arrived both she and Kim remained locked away in the bedroom. They were too afraid to leave it to answer the knock at the door. The police continued to ring the doorbell. They wrung it about six times before finally turning the door's handle that remained unlocked. As they made their way down the corridor Joyce came out of her room.

"Is everything okay in here?"

Kim finally got the nerve to peep out of the door.

"Here we are," Joyce said.

"Are you okay? Are you the person who called the station?"

"Yes we did," Joyce said.

"Did you see my other daughter out there anywhere?"

"No there was no one out front so we let ourselves in once we saw that the door was open. We were afraid that someone

175

maybe seriously injured," the officer said — explaining her action.

"Didn't you hear us ringing the door bell?"

"Yes we did. My daughters were fighting and my oldest daughter is just crazy... she's schizophrenic. She threw this ashtray and almost hit me on the side of my head," Joyce explained handing the officer the ashtray so that she could feel its weight.

"Where is she?" the officer inquired.

"She's in her room," Kim responded pointing across the hall to Felicia's bedroom.

"Come out of the room young lady!" The officer demanded. He knocked vigorously on Felicia's door with his flashlight. She exited the room with no resistance.

"What's the problem you seem to be having today young lady?"

"Do you see that lady over there? She thinks she's my mother... but she's not! Look at her! I'm twice her age. Look at her skin. She doesn't even look like me! How can she possible think that she could be my mother?"

"See... she's crazy," Joyce explained once again.

"I know this is your mother," the second officer said speaking for the first time. "Why are you acting up today?" He smiled at Felicia as if he were hoping to calm her. "You're too pretty of a lady to be acting like this. Look at your hair. It's so long and pretty. You'll be just fine." He tapped her gently on her shoulder.

"That's my daughter sitting in that chair," Felicia said pointing at Kim. "I raised that girl all by myself. Rats run up and down my fucking body everyday and night!" Felicia screamed. Her soft and low voice changed to a deep baritone. Her bright green eyes now turned a deep reddish-brown color.

"You want to see the rats! I'll show them to you… if you would like to see them!"

Her voice grew deeper and deeper. Her eyes opened wider and wider and with each word. She lifted her shirt up over her head and showing her breast. The officers, who appeared young and inexperienced, looked at one another in awe.

"You all will have to handle this in another way," one officer whispered. They then walked briskly out of the Tucker's home and without saying a word.

Kim and Joyce were yet again left alone to deal with Felicia. They went briskly back into the bedroom and locked the door. Minutes later they heard Felicia return to her room and she slammed the door.

Joyce telephones George — "I need you to come back home," she pleaded.

"What's wrong?"

"Felicia's at it again. I can't handle her! Please come home."

"I'm on my way," he promised.

Kim and Joyce remained in the room until he arrived. Although they hoped that the police would return to give them some kind of advice as to what to do with her — or to just check up on them.

George finally came home... "Open this door Felicia!" he demanded.

"Go away!"

George went and got his toolbox and removed Felicia's doorknob off the hinges.

"What is wrong with you girl? I can't even work without you acting up!"

Felicia didn't respond. She just lay innocently on the bed.

"What in the world is going on with her Joyce?"

Joyce explained to him how Felicia had thrown the ashtray that barely missed hitting her in the head. She told him all about the fight that she and Kim had that afternoon.

"I called the police and even they ran off," she told.

"What do you mean they ran off?"

"They ran off. They said that we will have to take care of this on our own," she explained.

"She must be worse off than I thought to have run the police away," George admitted.

"Can you imagine how I feel having to sleep in the same room with her for the past two years? She has driven me crazy," Kim told.

"Felicia, get dressed! I'm taking you to the hospital!"

"I'm already dressed and I'm not going to the fucking hospital!" she said.

"Joyce are you ready?"

"Yes," she said grabbing her coat.

Felicia put up a good commotion but George managed to get her out of the house and into the car.

"Well where is she?" Kim asked. She was astonished when Joyce and George returned without Felicia.

"They kept her at the hospital because she carried on so badly when we got there. She was fighting the doctors and the nurses. They had to put her in a straight jacket and they gave her a sedative to calm her down. She'll probably be there for a while."

Kim was so glad to see that Felicia would be getting the

179

help she knew she needed. She went into her bedroom and removed all the sheets from off Felicia's bed. The room reaped of smoke. She even removed the curtains from the windows and washed them. She washed down the mirrors with alcohol and the dressers with furniture polish. She hoped to remove Felicia's staled body odor. The sponge that she had used to clean the room was black as tar from the smoke residue when she was done. Even then she had to open the windows to get her scent out of the room.

Although Felicia remained in the hospital for a month Kim still didn't feel comfortable sleeping in her old bedroom. It reminded her so much of Felicia that she felt her presence even though she was not there. Kim went back to sleeping out on the sofa. The Tucker home was quiet once again and she was pleased to be getting the rest that she needed.

During the time that Felicia was away Kim found out that she was pregnant. All those nights she spent hanging out had finally caught up with her. She knew that she couldn't tell Joyce because she would tell George and he would put her in a girl's home. In desperation Kim went to Tessa's mother, Ms. Miriam, for help.

"Can you please take me to have an abortion?"

"No... I think you should talk to your mother."

"I can't because she'll kill me!"

"The best that I can do is to go over with you to talk to her. Come on and I'll drive you there," Ms. Miriam offered.

"Mom... I'm pregnant." Kim blurted it out after entering the house.

She felt confident because Ms. Miriam was there to support her and there was no other way to say it. So... Kim came straight out with it. Joyce didn't say a word.

Joyce burst into tears and ran into her bedroom where she stayed for hours. Joyce was like that sometimes, unpredictable and especially when she wasn't drinking.

"Well Kim I hope that everything goes well. I'll talk to you later," Ms. Miriam said.

"Thank you so much for coming with me," Kim said.

Later that afternoon Kim could hear Joyce talking on the telephone.

"I have a little money but I don't know how she'll get there. I certainly can't go with her and I don't plan on telling her father," Kim overheard her say.

From the conversation Kim realized that she was probably talking to Sassy or one of her other sisters in Washington. Just as she had finished her conversation Borne walked into the house.

"What's going on? Why is it so quiet in here?

Where's Mommy?" he asked Kim. She sat quietly on the sofa looking dumbfounded.

"Your sister has gotten herself knocked up. Do you think you can ride the bus with her to Washington so that she can get an abortion?"

"I could ride with her but I don't know my way around in Washington. I know this girl, Margaret, who lives up the street... she's from Washington. Perhaps she'll ride with her. Well that's if you pay her way on the bus."

"Go and ask her. I'll see if I can come up with the money. You're always getting into something! I don't know why you can't just sit your fast butt in the house."

Minutes later Borne and Margaret walked into the house.

"Hi Joyce. Yes I'll ride with your daughter to Washington," Margaret said. "I am twenty-seven with three children of my own.

I know that she does not want to be like me. When do you w me to take her?"

"I don't know how far along she is so if you can go tomorrow that would be great. Her sisters are making all the arrangements."

"Sure tomorrow's fine. I'll just go home and pack up my children things. I'll take them to my mother's house and she will keep them while I'm away."

"I really appreciate this Margaret. You are a nice girl to do this for people you barely even know."

"I know Borne very well," she said smiling.

"Oh, I see," Joyce said.

Kim sat there on the sofa and never said a word.

"It'll be okay," Margaret turned and said to her. "I know that the bus leaves around eight o'clock in the morning. I'll pick you up at seven o'clock."

"Okay," Kim said shyly.

"Go in the room and pack your things! I'll just have to tell your daddy that you are out of school a couple of days and that I sent you to spend some time with your sisters," Joyce said.

After Kim had packed her things she laid on the bed balled up in a knot. She remained there the rest of the evening. She didn't even come out to eat supper or to watch television. Margaret showed up at seven o'clock exactly. She and Kim were on the bus by seven-thirty. They had a two-hour layover in Virginia and arrived in Washington by three-thirty that afternoon.

Joyce had given Margaret Ginger's telephone number.

183

She was to telephone her once they arrived at the bus station. Arrangements were made to have Mr. Connie, a friend of Sassy, to pick them up. He was to drive Margaret to her family's house and to take Kim to Ginger's house.

Kim slept most of the evening and the following morning she was awaken by Ginger and driven to the abortion clinic. The procedure was performed. As she lay paralyzed on the table she endures the terror of her internal organs being suctioned and vacuumed. No care was given to the very existence which no longer cultivated inside of her being. When it was all finished Kim returned to Ginger's house where she rested up for two-days. They wanted to ensure that she was physically okay and that there were no complications. Margaret returned to get her and they returned to Rocking Barrel — as if they had never left the town.

Albeit this was an overwhelming ordeal for any fifteen-year old girl to tolerate — surely an experience that Kim would never forget. Once home Kim found that Felicia now portrayed a miraculous recovery. She appeared to be psychologically healed and had begun to take care of her personal hygiene. Her temper had quieted down tremendously. Showing evidence of remarkable improvement — Felicia's progress created vast talk in the Tucker's home of her returning to Washington. She would return to live with her other sisters. She continued to take her medicine regularly and seemed to be doing so much better.

One afternoon the doorbell rang and there stood Belinda, one of Felicia's old high school classmates stopping by to see her.

"Hi Kim. Look at you... you are all grown up now. I remember when Felicia and I used to change your diapers. Is Felicia home? I just found out that she was back in town and very sick. "

"Yes she's here... come on in and have a seat. I'll go get her."

"Okay," Belinda replied.

Kim went back to the back room where Felicia laid on the bed smoking her cigarettes.

"Felicia, Belinda is here to see you."

"Oh is she. Tell her I'll be right out in a minute."

"She'll be right with you in a moment Belinda."

"So how have you been doing Kim? You've turned into quite a beautiful young lady."

Kim and Belinda made small talk for about fifteen minutes and Felicia still had not come out of the room to join them.

"Let me go see what's keeping her."

"I hope it's not a bad time," Belinda said.

When Kim entered the bedroom Felicia was standing in the mirror putting on her make-up — which seemed to be thicker than usual.

"Are you coming out Felicia? Belinda's been waiting quite a while," she admitted. She hoped that this would put a fire to her and she would hurry.

"Yes, I'm coming," she responded. She exited the room.

"Hi Belinda," she said cheerfully. She gave Belinda a hug.

Kim watched in astonishment at the fact that Felicia actually sat there beside Belinda attempting to hold a descent conversation. For a moment it was surely like seeing the old, happy and fun loving Felicia back — the way she sat there smiling. She appeared to be enjoying Belinda's company.

Kim however was still not comfortable or trusting of this new and improved Felicia that stood before her. She sat with them for a while before joining Joyce in her room. Minutes after leaving the room she heard Felicia's voice.

"What did you say Bitch?"

Quickly Kim walked into the living room to see what was wrong.

"What did you say to me?" Felicia asked once again. Turning in circles and laughing whole-heartedly, looking away from everyone in the room. It was obvious that she had lost herself again.

"Whom is she talking to? What's wrong with her?"

"I have no idea. This is what she does every day. She was doing so much better when she first came home from the hospital. I was surprised that she even came out of her room to talk to you," Kim told Belinda.

"You think I'm crazy don't you. Well I'm not... you know I'm not. I'm as sane as you and her," she said now looking at Kim. "You're the one that's crazy," she said coming closer to Belinda. "Bitch you're not my friend! You've always been jealous of me because I'm prettier than you are! Now you come over here trying to be my friend."

"Get out! Get the HELL out!"

Belinda stood with tears in her eyes as she now rushed frantically towards the door.

"What happened to you Felicia? What in Heaven's Name has happened to you?"

"Why were you so rude to her?" Kim yelled in embarrassment. She just came over to see how you were doing. Why did you have to speak to her like that? I can't believe the way you treated her. I hope she never comes to visit you again! I know I wouldn't," Kim continued. "I hate you... I hate you!" she cried running out the door behind Belinda. "I'm sorry Belinda."

"Don't worry Kim. It isn't your fault. What's wrong with her? She used to be so sweet in school. God... how could this have happened to her. I've got to go. Perhaps I'll come again."

When Kim returned inside the house Felicia walked slowly down the corridor laughing deviously. Kim felt that she was laughing at her. Ignoring her Kim went back onto the porch where she sat thinking about the incident that had occurred with Belinda. She really felt bad for the way that Felicia had treated her and she would never forget the look of fear in Belinda's eyes. Kim had never been so embarrassed in her life and was certain that Belinda felt the same way that she did at that moment.

A couple of weeks after this ordeal Felicia asked George to buy her a pack of cigarettes. Of course he refused to buy them since he was a non-smoker. He didn't even buy Joyce cigarettes.

"You bastard!" Felicia swung at him forcefully, hitting him on his arm. George was so upset that he slammed her down onto the floor. Emotionless he pinned her down on to the floor. Not wanting to hurt her but trying to calm her psychotic behavior.

"This is it girl! I tried to give you a chance but now you have to go!" He dragged her out of the house to his car, by her wrists. Then he went to the trunk of his car to get some rope. He tired her hands together.

"What are you doing George? Put your shoes on Joyce. I'm taking her to the mental hospital again and this time I hope she'll never get out."

"I didn't know that she was that crazy," he said to Joyce when he returned home from the hospital. "Maybe we should have taken Kim's advice and gotten her some help sooner. She tried to tell us but we wouldn't listen. She has gotten worse. The Doctor said that it would require a lot of energy and time before she gets any better. Far more than we can ever give her," he confessed.

"Well now she's surely at the right place to get the help she needs," Joyce said.

Felicia's hospital stay was much longer lasting six months, if not more. Having stayed in the hospital so long, she gained so much weight from the medicines. Joyce had to buy her a new wardrobe. Her cheeks had gotten fat and her neck had a spontaneous twitch. Her head shook spontaneously back and forth uncontrollably.

"What is wrong with her?"

"She'll be all right... that's just a reaction from the medicine.

The doctor said that the side effects would subside once she gets use to the medicine."

Other than not having an appetite, Felicia was doing well on the medicine. She began to lose weight drastically going from 140 to 100 pounds, at the Height of 5'9.

Chapter 17

Kim stumbled upon her dear friend Stephen one afternoon when she was out with Tessa. She was stunned and surprised to see him. She had known him since the third grade and he now invited her to attend bible study with him.

"So what have you been doing Kim?"

"Nothing much... just hanging out with the girls."

"You should go with me to bible study on Wednesday?"

"What time Wednesday?"

"We meet at seven o'clock but I'll meet you at your house at six-thirty."

"Okay, I'll be glad to go with you."
She welcomed the opportunity to join him. He showed up at six-thirty exactly.

"Pastor Ron lives right up the street from my house. He is a good Pastor. I've been going to bible study for a year now."

When they arrived to the house there was no one there other than Kim and Stephen — of course Pastor Ron greeted them at the door.

"Brother Stephen I see you have brought a guess with you tonight."

"Yes this is Kim Tucker."

"Welcome Kim. Come on in here and have a seat. My wife, Jennifer and my daughters will be joining us in a minute or two."

Pastor Ron started the study out with a prayer and afterwards they began to read verses in the Bible. After they were done reading Pastor Ron began to preach. More than a bible study this was and very enlightening to Kim. She found it to be more like Sunday morning service and she enjoyed each moment. She and Stephen continued to attend the studies, every Wednesday night.

By the fourth week of attendance Pastor Ron spoke primarily on the discussion of Demons and how they often took possession of ones body. The more Kim took heed of the words of his sermon the more she began to associate it with Felicia. She was certain that this had to be what he was referring too. It was as though Pastor Ron was reading her mind. He seemed familiar with Felicia and the torment that Kim experienced at home. He seemed to give her guidance on how to protect herself from her.

"Keep your armor on. If you must... place the Bible next to your bed or under it then, do so. The Devil comes at you in so many directions and you have to be prepared."

After the sermon had ended Kim asked Stephen to wait for her outside on the porch. She wanted to speak further with Pastor Ron concerning her home situation with Felicia.

"Could I talk to you for a second?"

"Sure, Kim. What's on your mind?"

"My sister Felicia... I believe has a demon in her. She talks and laughs to herself constantly. She also threatens to kill me and daily. She is always saying that things like rats and snakes are crawling in and out of her body. She has to be possessed."

Kim could feel her entire body shake as she spoke to Pastor Ron. She now realized exactly how much Felicia's presence affected her soul.

"I can't take living with her anymore. You have got to come over and pray for her Pastor Ron."

She began to cry and released some of her deep-seated frustrations.

"Do not worry my child... it will be okay. I want you to go home now and I'll say a special prayer for you tonight. I want you and Stephen to come back tomorrow so that we can discuss this further. We will say another prayer at that time for you and your family."

Kim couldn't sleep that night. She was excited with anticipation of returning to Pastor Ron's home the following day. She and Stephen rushed there following school.

Immediately after entering the house Pastor Ron's wife escorted them hurriedly into the Prayer Room.

"Let's all kneel down for prayer," Pastor Ron requested of them and as they knelt he led them into prayer.

"I command that you Demons be removed from Felicia Tucker... this instance! In the Name of Jesus Christ our Lord and Savior — I demand you be gone from her!"

He prayed for Felicia and the release of all the Demons that Kim was certain had taken control of her mind and body. He continued to say the prayer repeatedly in the presence of the Lord as Stephen and Kim joined in giving confirmation to his distant exorcism.

Kim cried as he continued to pray. His words appeared to move over her like the sun fading into an overcast sky. Like his words, Pastor Ron moved slowly towards her. He put one hand on her forehead. "Bless Kim's home that she may find peace therein, In Jesus Name," he said with his words promising conviction.

She felt content and knew that very moment that everything

194

would now be okay as she cried and thanked the Lord confirming her blessing. After the prayer service had ended, Kim felt better. Having all faith and believing in her heart that her prayers had been answered.

"Damn Kim I didn't know that you were going through all of that turmoil with Felicia. Why didn't you tell me what you were going through at home? You know that you can talk to me about anything. I noticed that you haven't been your usual cheerful self. I had no idea that you were so sad or that Felicia was having such a negative impact on you. No wonder you seem to be so mentally preoccupied. I would have probably killed her by now if she were my sister," Stephen said while walking Kim home.

"I've thought about killing her. Believe me, I've thought about it a lot."

They were so engrossed in the praying for the cleanliness of Felicia's soul that time past so quickly. It was eleven o'clock when they arrived back at Kim's house and the lights were all out in the house. The house appeared dark and dreary — abandoned even. Although Kim was certain that everyone was asleep. She turned the doorknob on the front door however it was locked. Quite strange considering George rarely locked his doors unless all his children were securely in their beds.

Kim wrung the doorbell and unexpectedly seconds later Felicia opened up the door in a heated rage. She began to swing at Kim, hitting her in her face violently. Her swiftness in opening the door led Kim to believe that she had plotted the entire scene. Kim was certain that she stood at the door awaiting her arrival.

"I'm sick and tired of you and that damn Stephen Lax watching me every night! Why don't you people just leave me the hell alone? I'm not bothering you... so why do you insist on harassing me?"

Red with fury Kim now began to swing madly back at Felicia. Stephen grabbed her and pushed her behind him as to protect her from Felicia's wrath. Gently but firmly he grabbed her hands so that she would not swing at Felicia.

He tried to stop the fight and as he continued to hold on to Kim, Felicia continued to swing at her violently. Stephen began to back slowly off the porch leading Kim along the way with him. He tried not to trip over the steps as Felicia continued to come towards them. Looking baffled at each other Stephen and Kim were uncertain as to why Felicia was so agitated with them.

What could she have possibly meant by the fact that they were harassing her," Kim thought.

"What is your problem? You have lost your mind! Stay away from me!" Kim yelled.

"Do you know what sin you have performed against me?" Felicia yelled at Kim returning into the house, slamming and locking the door behind her.

"Good-bye Stephen," Kim said.

She walked back onto the porch and rung the doorbell, yet again. She hoped that this time George or Joyce would open the door. She didn't want to have another altercation with Felicia. Although she had said her farewell to Stephen, he stood there waiting for someone to open the door. The living room light shined through the window and Kim knew that her George was coming to her rescue. He always turned on the corridor light before answering the doorbell.

"What is going on out here?"

"Felicia's possessed and I am bringing the preacher here tomorrow to pray for her."

"This is my damn house and there will be no preacher coming to do anything to anyone unless I approve of it... and I tell you I don't approve of it! Get in this house right now! Where have you been anyway?"

"I've been at Bible Study," she stated closing the door behind her.

While getting her sheets and blanket out of her hall closet Kim noticed that Felicia had closed her bedroom door. In her anger she wanted to rush to curse her out for having attacked her the way that she had done. She stood restlessly wondering could Felicia have been in a rampage because of the prayer service that they had held in her honor that evening.

She had to have been angry about the prayer service... what else could have brought about such evil in her? She and Stephen hadn't awakened her; it appeared that she had been awaiting their arrival... her having opened the door so quickly, Kim thought.

Kim went into the bathroom where she knelt down on her knees and began to pray. She prayed for Felicia as well as for her George. She felt now that he too was evil, as well as Felicia. She believed that they both were possessed. George had come off so quickly in Felicia's defense becoming agitated and disliked the idea of Kim inviting Pastor Ron into their home. She remained there on her knees and in prayer asking God to help her through this tremendous situation that she couldn't handle.

In fear of Felicia's wrath she lay there on the bathroom floor balled up in a knot. She used her hands as a pillow and slept there all night behind the locked door. In the morning after

198

showering she came out of the bathroom where she found Felicia standing in the Kitchen. She was quite surprised to see that she had cooked breakfast.

"Do you want something to eat?" she asked Kim.

She acted as if they had never had an altercation that prior night.

"No thank you," Kim replied.

She sat down in the living room on the sofa and began to read her Bible. She waited until Felicia had left the kitchen and went to fix herself a bowl of cereal. She refused to eat Felicia's cooking. Felicia became much nicer to Kim following their confrontation and Kim was certain that it was because she didn't want her to bring Pastor Ron into their home.

Stephen and Kim continued to go to Bible study and to spend time together. Stephen's sister, Wanda would take them to the movies and pick them up afterwards. Soon their friendship had blossomed into somewhat of a relationship.

They began sitting in the theater holding hands and sometimes kissing passionately.

One night after the movie, Wanda invited Kim to spend the night over at Stephen's house with them since their mother was out of town. Kim agreed innocently not knowing that Stephen had his own plans for the affair. On the way there, they stopped by to pick up Wanda's boyfriend William. He hopped into the car and off they went to Stephen's house. They played cards until late in the night and finally the time had come to go to bed.

"I'll get you a night gown, Kim," Wanda said.

"Okay."

"I'll take this end of the bed," Kim said.

"Oh, William is sleeping with me. You can sleep in with Stephen."

Kim's eyes widen at the idea of sleeping with Stephen. The thought had never crossed her mind that the two of them would be sharing a bed. She cared for Stephen deeply but in a strange and peculiar way. He was a nice guy whom she enjoyed spending time with however she didn't love him the way that he loved her. Her love for him was more like a brotherly love and not that of a wife. Stephen was constantly asking her to marry him. She loved the fact that she could express her deepest thoughts and feelings to him. Being with him; to Kim, was somewhat like spending time with Jessica or Leslie.

"Okay," Kim said, cheerfully trying relentlessly not to display her uneasiness to Wanda.

"Come on Kim, my room is back here," Stephen said.

As she exited the room, her legs shook nervously. She passed William in the corridor as he so proudly entered Wanda's bedroom. Stephen now stood facing her as she stood about awkwardly. He stretched out his hands towards her and she grasped his hands holding on so tightly.

Astonishingly that in that very moment Kim saw Stephen in a different light. She now viewed a man standing in front of her and not some boyish childhood friend. Against her better judgment, she lay next to him enjoying each moment of his kissing and caressing her. That evening as his gentle soft touches continued, they made breathtaking love. She remained engrossed in his arms until sunrise.

"I love you Kim," Stephen said sincerely kissing her tenderly across her eyebrow. She lay content entwined in his arms.

It was at that moment in which Kim had second thoughts. She began to wonder in uncertainty as to whether she had made the right choice by making love to him. As she lay in aspiration she hoped that their actions would not ruin their friendship. She quietly watched him as he slept so peacefully.

Feeling awkward and somewhat ashamed of her actions

the following morning, she lay there teasingly beside him pretending to be asleep. Stiffening her body as Stephen jumped elatedly up out of the bed and onto the floor. She didn't say a word or acknowledge the fact that she was awake.

"Good morning sweetheart," he whispered softly. He kissed her ear gently sending an arousing feeling briefly through her body. "What would you like for me to cook you for breakfast?" he asked.

"Anything you prepare will be fine with me," she expressed wearing a smile of brightness and satisfaction.

She sprung up out of the bed and followed him into the kitchen.

He began preparing scrambling eggs, grits, bacon and toast for not only her but also for Wanda and William. They had not yet come up for air. After demolishing their breakfast, Wanda offered to take Kim home.

"I will give you a call later on this afternoon," he said to Kim. William accompanied them as Stephen remained home cleaning the dishes.

"You've just made him the happiest boy in Rocking Barrel," Wanda insisted, giggling softly.

"Why do you say that?"

"You are all he every talks about. He adores you," she confided.

202

A guilty feeling came over Kim. She knew that she didn't have those same feelings for Stephen. There was no way she would tell this to his sister. She sat there quietly, holding her secret inside and never said a word. She felt more so now that she had made a major mistake. Genuinely he meant the world to her. She never wanted to loose the bond they shared. Nonetheless, she didn't have such deep feelings for Stephen.

Returning home to the sound of the telephone ringing, she rushed to answer its ring. Her heart gave somewhat of a murmur when she heard Stephen's voice on the other end of the receiver. Having second thoughts about what they had done, she now knew that their friendship would not be the same. She knew now that she had made a mistake by sleeping with Stephen.

"I'm going to finish a couple more tasks around the house and afterwards, I'll take a shower and then I plan to come over. You can expect me there around four o'clock," he said.

"Sure. I'll see you when you get here," she said.

In anticipation of his arrival, she felt a little tense and nervous about seeing him for the first time since their sexual encounter. She became a little flustered with his conversation when he first arrived because he kept saying how much he loved her.

"Will you marry me, Kim?" he asked.

Please relax Stephen, I told you a dozen times that we are too young to be discussing marriage! Granted, last night was a pleasure and I cherish our relationship. Please let's not mess up our friendship by making more of last night. I don't want to get married and you're forcefulness causes me to feel a little regretful and uncomfortable around you.

Let's try to revitalize our friendship and get it back to where it was, before last night.

He stood, heartbrokenly, facing Kim with his eyes full of tears. Looking somewhat boyishly, he stared into her eyes as she now felt that she had betrayed her best friend.

"Kim, you know I have profound feelings for you and I must admit that I always have. Since the first day I laid eyes on you. I knew you were the one for me, even then. I can't imagine you being with anyone other than me and I was certain that you felt the same way about me."

Somewhat embarrassed as Stephen's charmed won her heart Kim whispered softly to him, "I love you too Stephen. Truthfully, I do... but, not as deeply or even in the same respect as you," she admitted disappointedly. "I apologize for my bluntness but I feel I must be honest with you and not misleading."

Kim confessed her true feelings with comfort as she had done so often with him.

"I think we shouldn't see each other for a while and maybe give our relationship some thought."

She attempted to walk slowly away from him.

"Me not see you anymore: unthinkable." How could you even suggest such a thing?"

He grabbed her forcefully by her arm and pulled her back towards him. "There is no way that I can ever stop being with you. You are my life: Kim, you mean the world to me."

"As disappointing as it maybe to you Stephen, I must admit that I feel that our lovemaking has ruined the closeness of our relationship. I feel that we need to be apart from one another and deal with this change in our lives. I'm sorry but we should. At least until we can both sort out true feelings? I'm sorry but my feelings for you are a little cloudy right now."

"If you need time alone to think things through, then I'll give you that time. I just don't want there to be any unsettled feelings between you and I," he shared.

"Please give me just a little time." She hugged him tightly in her arms; hoping to ease the hurt, which showed upon his face.

"Okay, I'll give you your time. Call me when you're ready to see me again." He walked away from Kim, with his head hung sorrowfully downward. He turned briefly to get a final glimpse of her.

"Sure, I will call you." Kim was content now that she had finally gotten her true feelings out in the open.

She realized that romancing Stephen, her best friend, was the worst thing that she had ever done. She was sorrowful to lose his friendship. She knew that she would miss their open conversations and his deep sincerity. Quite heartbreaking for her but she had no other choice. She hoped that he would one day forgive her and that they could rekindle their friendship at some point in life.

When the summer ended, Kim decided to enroll herself into a new school. She did this hoping to ease Stephen's hurt and because didn't want anything distracting her from her studies. Especially since this was her senior year of high school. The weeks went by at high-speed and she finally felt as though she had a new start on life. Despite the fact that she now had a ten mile walk to school each morning, Kim was happy. The walk alone seemed to give her the opportunity to get Felicia and Jason out of her head. The old skeletons seemed far behind her now.

She excelled rapidly the first two quarters at her new school since she was able to stay focused.

No longer was she distracted by the whispers she often heard in the corridor of her old school,

"There's Kim Tucker, you know... the one who got raped her sophomore year. She's as crazy as her sister Felicia."

She remained quite content for a while however her grades began to lag behind by third quarter. Once again, she began to feel the stress at home as Felicia's mental state continued to deteriorate.

She knew that if she remained in that God forsaken Rocking Barrel that she would never graduate. If she stayed, she too would go insane. The mere idea of laying her head down to sleep at night had become a burden.

Finally, all the praying that she had done began to pay off when Tessa re-entered into her life.

"Hey Tessa, what are you doing here?"

"I'm switching over to this school."

"That's wonderful, I'm sure that you are going to love it here. I hope that you will be placed in my class room."

However, they were not placed in any of the same classes but Kim and Tessa began hanging out together once again. Kim would stay over at Tessa's house, frequently. Especially in the winter, or when the news forecasts anticipated rain. Tessa's house was closer to school and she didn't have to walk as far.

"Tessa, do you think that your mother would let me move in with you?"

"Move in with us. Why in the world would you want to move in with us? You know that your parents are not going to let you leave home until after you graduate."

"I have got to get out of that house. It is evil — Felicia's evil and I can't take living with her another minute! I feel as though I am going insane."

"Could you please just ask her?"

"I'll ask her but I don't think that she will agree with letting you stay."

"Ms. Miriam, please let me come here to live with you and Tessa? This way I can be closer to school?" Kim was certain that Ms. Miriam would let her stay. She was so certain, that she didn't wait for Tessa to ask her but instead she blurted it out herself.

"Why do you want to come live here? I can barely take care of my own children. I couldn't afford to feed another stomach."

"Please let me stay with you Ms. Miriam. I promise not to

be a burden on you. I can help Tessa out with the cooking, cleaning and even looking after the children. I hate my house! It's evil! If I don't get away from that Felicia, I'm sure to go crazy!"

"You have got to be crazy already, if you want to come here to live. Who is Felicia?"

"Felicia's my schizophrenic sister. Come to my house... you'll see the madness. Felicia is a lunatic. There is no doubt about it — she's mad. You'll see why I have to get away from her."

"Okay, let's go. I have to meet this Felicia. Well, are you two coming?" Ms. Miriam grabbed her purse and headed towards the door. Kim and Tessa followed her to the car, astonished at the fact that she was actually going to Kim's house.

"Mom, I have someone here whom I would like for you to meet," Kim said as they entered the house. "This is Ms. Miriam, Tessa's mom."

"It's a pleasure to finally get the chance to meet with you. Kim has told me so much about you. She has practically moved in with you."

"That's what brings me here. Surprisingly enough, she asked me today, if she could come to stay with us. I told her that it was out of the question but promised that I would talk to you about it."

"Kim, knows that she can't put herself on you like that. I don't know what has gotten into her lately. I'm sorry that she would ask you such a foolish thing."

"It's quite all right with me and it would only be during the wee Actually, I don't mind if she does come to stay with us. She has really been a great help around the house helping Tessa with keeping the house clean. They watch after the younger two children. I work at night and it's good to know that I don't have to worry about them while I'm working. I wanted to get a feel of your thoughts on the matter."

Kim and Tessa sat quietly while their Parents spoke to one another as if they had known each other for years. Felicia entered the room, as if to make an entrance.
Ms. Miriam watched closely as Felicia slid her way across the room. She sat down on the sofa and pierced her eyes on the ceiling.

"I don't know. I would have to talk to Kim's father to see what he thinks about her staying with you. I'll let you know what he says tomorrow."

"Bitch... she's nothing but a fucking bitch!" Felicia shrieked.

"Felicia, don't you see that we have company. Go back in your room with that mess!" Joyce urged.

"I hate you! I hate you! You fucking bitch!" Felicia looked at Ms. Miriam directly in her face as she passed her path on the way to her room.

"Is she talking to me?"

"No, please ignore her. That's my daughter Felicia. I'm sure that Kim has told you all about her. "

"Yes, she has. She said that she was part of the reason why she wanted to live with us. What a temper that girl has. Is she angry like that often?"

"Everyday, she goes on a rampage."

"You have patience. I certainly couldn't deal with that behavior and would have to have her committed."

"She's fine if she takes her medicine. The problem is getting her to take it."

"Well, let me know what your husband says. We would love to have Kim to come stay. She is definitely no bother. It's supposed to rain in the morning. She can stay tonight, if it's okay with you."

"Yes, she can stay tonight."

Kim went in the back and packed her clothes and they were back off to Tessa's home.

"I'll see you tomorrow when I drop Kim back off," Ms. Miriam said, minutes before Felicia violently, opened and slammed her bedroom door.

"You were right Kim. I don't know how you could stay there with that Felicia. You're parents really do need to get her some help."

That very night, Joyce called Miriam to say that she and George agreed to let Kim come to live with her.

"We haven't been able to do a thing with her since Felicia arrived. Perhaps this will be better for her."

Kim was at peace again at Tessa's house, with Ms. Miriam and the rest of the family. She was quite concerned when one afternoon Ms. Miriam came home to say that she would be leaving.

"I trust that the two of you will take care of the younger children while I'm away."

Months went by and Ms, Miriam came home one morning and said.

"Away... where are you going?" Tessa asked.

"I've decided to move in with Bruce. He's asked me to marry him. You are seventeen now and Marcus is twenty-one. I think that you can take care of yourselves."

"Well what about Tara and Karen, Mom?" Marcus asked.

"You and Marcus can take care of them while I'm away," she said. "I also trust that you won't have any boys running! You don't want to be a bad influence on the younger children."

Ms. Miriam chose to move across town to live with her boyfriend. She continued to pay the mortgage intrusting that Tessa and her older brother, Marcus, would make the payments and take care of the children.

Tessa and Marcus remained very responsible that first month following Ms. Miriam's departure from the home. However, the next month Marcus decided that he was moving out of the home as well, leaving Tessa all alone to take care of the house and her younger sisters. She and Kim would come home from school to prepare supper for Tessa's two younger sisters. They tried to be responsible teenagers in taking care of the household.

Tessa performed most of the cooking while Kim did the majority of the house cleaning chores. This system worked perfectly well for the two girls who were getting along fantastically. Each day after supper, they requested that the younger girls complete their homework. Afterwards, they ensured that the girls ironed their clothes for school the following day. While engrossed in their ironing, Kim and Tessa would sit in the room and checked over their homework.

Rapidly the rumor spread around town about Tessa and Kim having full access to Miriam's house while she was away. Nikki and Marcel two of their classmates began coming home with them almost daily. This was so often that it was as if they had two extra mouths to feed. Of course, this was not an issue or problem especially since Ms. Miriam brought the groceries.

"Gosh, you all have been eating a substantial amount of food lately," Ms. Miriam acknowledged one afternoon when she came by to visit. "What... am I feeding an Army? Are you two living here, too?" She asked this of Nikki and Marcel who sat quietly at the table.

"No, we're not living here," they echoed in sequence to Ms. Miriam's question.

Tessa and Kim were somewhat glad that Ms. Miriam had confronted Nikki and Marcel because they were not quite sure how to bring up the touchy conversation. Tessa and Kim had been trying to suffice by cooking smaller portions and sharing their portions with Nikki and Marcel and leaving the remainder for Tessa's younger sisters.

Chapter 18

Rightfully bored out of their minds from babysitting everyday Tessa and Kim began to hang out at the nightclub. They partied Thursday thru Sunday. Tessa would often call Marcus over to look after her sisters while she, Kim, Nikki and Marcel would go exploring the club. Ms. Miriam had even started to let Tessa drive her car but only after dropping her off to work on her evening shift. She and Kim would return to pick her up in the morning and on their way to school.

Kim, Tessa, Nikki and Marcel were now party animals. This is how Kim met Ricardo. He was four years older than her and had recently returned to Rocking Barrel after graduating from a two-year business college. In less than a month Kim had fallen madly in love with him. She became so mesmerized by him that she began to spend less time with Tessa, Marcel and Nikki. She spent all of her time with him.

"You and Ricardo's relationship is going to get stale if you continue to spend all your time together. Every time I turn around there he is knocking on the door. You ought to be worn out from the mere idea of looking at him every day," Tessa said.

"Really you should," Marcel said sarcastically, showing her approval and agreement with Tessa's accusation.

215

"I know one thing… I have had it up to here with the two of you! That's all you talk about is Ricardo. Nikki raised her hands up above her head to show the length of her frustration. She and laughed hysterically.

"Okay, okay that's real funny! You all are just jealous because you don't have anyone knocking on the door for you." Just as she finished speaking, there was a knock on the door.

"Speak of the devil," Tessa said sarcastically. She knew the knock to be that of Ricardo.

Excitedly, Kim went running to the door as she too anticipated and hoped that it was Ricardo. Although knowing that her girlfriends were not as fond of him as she was. "Please don't disrespect him," she requested before opening the door nervously.

"Hi sweetie come on in," Kim insisted. She gave Ricardo a passionate kiss on his lips knowing that this would agitate her girlfriends even more.

"Hello ladies," he said addressing Nikki, Marcel and Tessa, who eyed him down like a bunch of wild cats; giving him the cold shoulder as he entered the room. They refused to respond to his sincere greeting and chose not to acknowledge his presence.

"Is there a problem?" he asked in frustration.

"Just ignore them, Ricardo. They have their asses upon their shoulders today! So are you ready to go?" Kim was embarrassed by her friends' impetuous attitudes.

"Bring your things and let's go," Ricardo insisted.

Kim went in the back room, packed a couple of outfits and she rushed out of the door behind him.

"Why didn't you pack all of your things?"

"What do you mean all of my things?"

"Well you know I got my tax refund today and I thought that you and I could move into one of the hotel rooms for a week." He refreshed her memory back to their previous conversation.

Kim felt a little nervous and anxious about moving to the hotel with Ricardo but she went back inside Tessa's house to pack the rest of her clothes.

Having gotten the cold shoulder from her friends she decided that it was best that she took Ricardo up on his offer. She moved with him into a hotel room. She would much rather spend time alone with him, instead of drinking herself to sleep tirelessly every night with her girlfriends. She also hoped that she could concentrate more on her schoolwork. School was a very important part of Kim's life.

She knew that Ricardo would take good care of her, especially since he worked as a technician at one of the local automotive shops. There was no doubt in her mind that he could afford the $100.00 a week tab in which the hotel charged. She also truly thought that Ricardo was her soul mate.

There she enjoyed the nights she lay in his arms. Often they sat alone in the peaceful room, never finding the time to argue. The two were much too busy making love all night.

The first month that they were in the room, Ricardo had no problem getting Kim a ride to and from school. However, shortly thereafter, they found it hard to depart from one another each morning. Kim began missing days from school and him from work. They lay recklessly in the room. They didn't consider their futures as they savored each moment of their intense lovemaking.

It was not long before Kim was playing full-time wife. She began skipping her morning classes as well as her afternoon classes. Often, she felt weak from exhaustion, having been up until the wee hours of the morning engrossed in Ricardo. She no longer cared about her English and Math classes in which she desperately needed to graduate. Kim enjoyed Business Law class, so much, that she ensured that she didn't miss a single day of class. She slept in late every morning and got up two-hours before her afternoon class to study. She would wait patiently on Ricardo to pick her up on his lunch break and drop her off at school. This love affair continued until Ricardo received his termination notice from his job.

"You have been coming in late every other day, or some days not at all. We need a dependable employee," Ricardo's boss said.

"I guess you'll have to move back home or back with Tessa. I would prefer it if you moved back home," Ricardo then suggested to Kim.

"I can't get to school from home," Kim told.

"I'll come by and pick you up in the mornings and take you back home after school," he promised.

With his promise and at his request, Kim moved back home, with Felicia but not for long. A month later, she returned to Tessa's house. Marcel and her boyfriend, Dexter, were now living in the house with Tessa.

One afternoon having heard a loud horn blowing outside the house, Kim rushed to the door hoping to see Ricardo. However, she was disappointed to find that it was not he at the door.

"Tessa, who is this guy parked out side of the house and

why is his car making all of that noise?"

"It's Brian and that's his muffler."

His muffler, you could hear throughout the house.

"Is Tessa home?" he asked with a thick, deep southern accent.

"I don't believe so, let me see," Kim said.

She went in the back room, where Tessa was changing her clothes. Brian began to blow his horn loudly, which over showered the sound of the loud roaring muffler.

"Wait a minute I'm coming!" Tessa yelled at him out the door.

"Who is this Brian, Tessa?" Kim asked.

"That's just Brian come on... let's go," she said. She grabbed Kim's arm and pulled her out to his car. Marcel and Dexter came running out of the door quickly behind them.

"Where are we going?"

"We're going to the club; get in the car."

"Do I have to?" She held her nose to escape the strong urine smell that filled the air in the car.

Brian got out of the car and walked over to the passenger's side to open the door for Tessa.

"When are you going to get this loud muffler fixed?" Tessa asked.

Kim eyed the nappy-headed thirty-something-year old man as he walked around the car to the passenger's seat. He wore a red and blue, wide collared cotton plaid-shirt. He also wore wide legged, tan, black and polyester pants. He wore black leathered like stacked shoes. His eyes were dark and beady like a crow. Kim figured if he was taller and seventy-pounds heavier, that he would have been the gruesome image of Jason. This of course was not at all pleasing to her.

When they arrived at the club, Brian handed Tessa a twenty-dollar bill as they all got out of the car. He turned the radio up loud and stayed behind out in the car.

"Isn't he going to come in too?" Kim asked.

"Are you crazy? No there is no way he is going in there with me. He's going to sit right out here in his car and wait for us," Tessa said.

"You're kidding."

"No, I'm not. He does it all the time and he'll take us home as soon as the club is closed."

"Where did you find him?" Kim asked.

Tessa paid each of their way in the club with the twenty dollar bill that Brian had given her.

After partying at the club they returned to the car where Brian lay across the front seat asleep. Tessa banged on the window. As usual and robotically he sat up and unlocked the doors to let them into the car.

"Why is the seat wet? Did you wet on yourself again Brian?"

"No, I didn't wet on myself. I spilled beer."

Tessa jumped out of the front seat and got in the back seat with the others.

"That's what you always say — but your car always smells like urine," Tessa said.

Although Kim had fun in the club, she now realized that it was high time that she retired from the club scene. She would be turning seventeen that summer and felt that it was time to grow up.

As she looked out the window, she considered Ricardo. She wondered how he had spent his evening. She had not seen much of him since they no longer lived in the hotel room. Having become engrossed with Tessa and her friends once again, she had somewhat forgotten about him. The only time that she had seen him was when he picked her up and took her home from school, the month that she was living at home.

She called him immediately after awakening the following morning to get an update report on his whereabouts.

"Hey, Ricardo... it's me."

"Yeah I know it's you, Kim."

"So, where have you been?"

"What do you mean where have I been? I've been home. Where have you been is the question."

"You moved back over there with Tessa and I didn't hear a word from you," he said.

"I've only been back here for a week. You weren't coming by my house to see me, so why should I just sit around with Felicia? Even before I moved back over here, I only saw you on the weekends. You've changed a lot and that is really unlike you."

"I've been out looking for employment. Besides, you and I both know that I need to make some money. We can't be together without money. That is what you want — isn't it?"

"Yes, that is what I want but I do not see why you can't at least stop over to say hello every once in a while. Money isn't everything you know and I don't want to move back into one of those rooms."

"Money isn't everything but we can't live without it."

"So when am I going to see you?"

"I don't know... just give me some time."

"Okay," Kim said. Feeling disappointed, she hung up the telephone.

Ricardo didn't call her back as she expected and she didn't call him. Instead, she hadn't seen Nikki in months and now wondered how she was doing. She gave her a call since Ricardo had insisted on her giving him some time to himself.

"What are you doing Nikki?"

"Hey Kim, how have you been? I can't believe you are calling. You mean to tell me that Ricardo let you up for some air?"

"Girl, I'm doing okay considering that Ricardo just told me that he needs a break from me."

"A break, what's that? He wasn't saying that when the two of you were laid up in that hotel for all of those months."

"He claims that he is looking for a job."

"Well I don't think that he is going to find a job on a Sunday."

"My mother is on her way to work. I'll ask her to drop me off at your house. If that's okay with you?"

"Yeah, you can come by," Kim said.

When Nikki arrived, they sat out on the front porch where they talked for hours. Kim realized just how much she had missed spending time with Nikki. There conversation came to an abrupt halt by the ringing of the telephone. To Kim's surprise, it was Ricardo calling that evening.

"Hi Kim, what are you doing."

"Not much, Nikki's over and we were just about to walk down to the store to get some beer."

"Nikki, oh yeah, I remember her. Do you think that she would be interested in meeting my friend Steve?"

"I don't know. She's not seeing anyone at this time so she may be interested. Let me ask her."

"Nikki, Ricardo wants to know if you are interested in meeting one of his friends."

"Who is he?"

"I don't know. Ricardo... Nikki wants to know who he is," Kim relayed.

"She can find that out when she meets him. Just tell her that his name is Steve."

"Ricardo said you can get all those details after you two have met," Kim replied. He said that his name is Steve."

"Steve... well I don't see any reason for me not to meet Steve," Nikki replied.

"Ricardo, she said yes, she'll meet Steve," Kim told."

"Okay, we're on our way over."

"I'll see you when you get here," Kim said.

Nikki and Kim waited anxiously for their arrival.

"Anything is better than sitting on the porch," Nikki said.

When they arrived Ricardo introduced Nikki to Steve and the four of them decided to go to the movies. Nikki and Steve took to one another right away. After the movies they sat in the back seat of Steve's car and kissed and held hands as if they had known one another for years. Kim thought back to a year ago when she first met Ricardo at the nightclub. There relationship too was love at first sight.

"Slow down back there," Ricardo said.

"Shut up and mind your business!" Steve yelled.

After that night the four of them hung out together constantly. Ricardo got a job working with Steve at the manufacturing shop. On the weekends, the couples met at the hotel where they got adjourning rooms.

The fun that she had been having with her friends came to an abrupt halt when Joyce was admitted into the hospital and diagnosed with sclerosis of the liver. The thought of losing her mother frightened her greatly. The seriousness of her illness sent Kim into a deep state of depression. She began to spend less time with her friends and spending more time at home.

After a month past she began to hear rumors that Ricardo was seeing Nikki's friend, Vinita.

"I noticed you eating lunch with Nikki. I can't believe you're still speaking to her after what she and Vinita did last night," Renee, Ricardo's younger sister said to Kim.

"What are you talking about, Renee? What did they do last night?"

"Well late last night I over heard Ricardo talking on the telephone to my cousin Maurice. I heard them discussing how the two of them had run a train on Nikki and Vinita."

"I don't believe you. I just saw Nikki and Vinita today in the lunchroom and they were all over me pretending to be my friends. Vinita even invited me to her birthday party," Kim told.

"Are you going to go?"

"Yes, I plan to go," Kim said spitefully.

"Why are you going to go to her party? What are you going to do, Kim?"

"I'm not certain yet. I know that Ricardo, Marcus and Nikki

227

will all be there so maybe I'll go to see how they'll react to my presence."

"You're going to confront her at her birthday party?"

"I didn't say that. I don't know what I am going to do.

I just wan to see their faces when I stroll into the room."

"Do you think that you can give me a ride?"

"Sure I will." Although Ricardo had not called Kim in weeks, he called here the Friday night before the party.

"Hey Kim, what are you going to be doing tomorrow night?"

"Oh nothing... I'll probably just sit around the house. I wanted to take you to see a movie.

"What time will you be picking me up?"

"I'll be there about ten o'clock." Minutes later the telephone wrung one again and it was Renee calling for Kim.

"I heard Ricardo asking you to go out to the movies with him tomorrow night. I hope you realize that this was only a plot to stop you from going to the party. Do you still want me to pick you up tomorrow?"

"I'll call you, Renee... that's if Ricardo doesn't show up by ten-thirty."

"He's not going to show-up, Kim."

"I'll call you," Kim said.

Kim waited for Ricardo until eleven o'clock that following evening. She called Renee, who answered the telephone after one ring.

"Could you come get me, Renee?"

"I'm on my way!" She was at Kim's house in less than fifteen minutes.

Kim and Renee could hear the sound of slow music playing as they approached the house that was fully packed. People occupied each corner of the house. They slow danced to the music. Kim looked anxiously for Ricardo however she didn't see him or Vinita. As she viewed the room further she saw Ricardo over in a corner holding Vinita tightly in his arms. She watched them as he kissed her passionately, pulling her closely to his body. In a jealous rage, she rushed across the room.

"What do you think you're doing Ricardo? Vinita how could you pretend to be my friend when all the while you were romancing Ricardo behind my back!"

"Ricardo loves me," Vinita said.

Kim grabbed her by her shirt.

"What are you doing Kim? Let her go!"

Ricardo grabbed Kim by the arm and pulled her out of the house.

"What did you think you were doing in there? There's nothing going on between me and Vinita."

"What do you think I'm blind?"

"What are you talking about?"

"Renee told me all about you, Maurice, Vinita and Nikki going to the hotel!" Ricardo had no response to Kim's allegations.

"Are you coming back inside Ricardo?" Vinita asked.

"No, he's going to take me home," Kim said.

"Come on Ricardo... come back into the party," Vinita taunted.

"Just take me home and I don't want to see you again!" Kim insisted to Ricardo.

"Okay, come on," he said without hesitation.

He took her home and she got out of the car and slammed the door.

Chapter 19

She began to get back into school and was very excited that military recruiters were coming to her school. The rain continued to pour upon her life as Joyce was rushed back to the hospital, once again. She was suffering from sclerosis of the liver. Although this appeared to be the worst segment of Kim's life, she remained optimistic. She prayed that Joyce would return home in time to see her walk across the stage to receive her diploma.

As graduation rapidly approached, Kim had no idea as to what life had to bestow upon her. Therefore, she felt no need or point in attending her graduation ceremony. She contemplated not going all day and at the last minute, she decided that it was to her best interest to attend. With none of her family members attending the affair... she felt useless. Joyce remained hospitalized and George showed no interested in attending.

Once there, Kim walked shyly across the stage as her name was called. She stood with confidence. Content with the diploma she now held tightly in her hands she believed would open many doors for her. Her classmates had their lives all planned. Many were to join the military and others planned to go off to college. Kim however had no idea what she was going to do now that she had graduated.

She called Ginger the following morning.

"Hey Ginger it's me... Kim."

"Hey Kim... congratulations! You're the last Tucker child to graduate! What are your plans now that you have completed your high school education?"

"I haven't given much thought about what I'm going to do but I know that I want to get out of Rocking Barrel. I was kind of hoping that I could come up there to live with you."

"Sure. Come whenever you like. You have my okay to come here to live."

"Great! You know I can't come until mother gets home from the hospital. It's nice to know that I will be eventually able to get out of here."

"Just call me when you're ready to come."

"Okay... I'll talk to you again soon," Kim said as she hung up the telephone.

"Can you go to the store to get me some cigarettes?" Felicia yelled from the back room.

"Sure I'll go," Kim replied.

She was filled with pleasure at the fact that Ginger had agreed to let her come to Washington. As she walked leisurely down the street to the store, she heard a loud car horn blowing from the rear of her. She turned quickly thinking she was in the car's path. To her delight and quite a pleasurable surprise, it was Maverick. He sat flamboyantly behind the wheel of a turquoise blue sports car appearing quite advantageous.

"Hey, where have you been?" He yelled.

"I've been around. Where have you been is more like it.

Jessica and I thought that you just fell off the face of the earth."

"I've been in the Army for the past seven years."

"Are you going back for good?"

"I'm back for right now... I'll probably re-enlist. What are you doing on this side of town?

"Well I live right up the street, I was on my way to the store to pick up a pack of cigarettes for my sister."

"Get in and I'll give you a ride."

"Great, why not — it's very muggy out here today." Kim offered mild flirtation, elevating her skirt slightly above her knees as she got into the car.

"Yes, it is very hot," Maverick, said in agreement now looking down at Kim's muscular legs. "I see you've worked up a sweat," he said handing her a napkin.

"Yes, a slight one." Kim laughed as she got out of the car to go into the store. Maverick waited out side of the store for her return.

"Do you have any plans for this evening?" he asked.

He turned towards her and their eyes met for the first time in a long time.

"No, I don't have any plans."

"You mean to tell me that a sexy young lady such as yourself is staying home on a Saturday night? You don't have a boyfriend to wine and dine you?"

"Not at this time."

"Wonderful, then I can come take you out tonight?"

"Sure, I don't see why not."

"I'll see you at eight o'clock," he said.

Kim got out of the car. She turned slowly to see his glossy white teeth shining magically below his full, juicy lips.

"Okay, I'll see you tonight."

She handed Felicia her cigarettes and ran anxiously through the house fumbling through her closet to find the perfect outfit to wear. She was so wound up about seeing Maverick once again! She was even more astonished that he had invited her on a date. Kim tried on several outfits before she finally decided what she would wear. She chose her red mini-skirt with a matching red body shirt. She also decided to take her favorite black silk jacket because the whether often got chilly in the evening hours in Rocking Barrel. This was the perfect outfit for any occasion. The jacket and Maverick would keep her warm if he chose to take her to the movies.

Kim was tickled with the fact that Maverick arrived earlier than eight o'clock. He was on time and not a minute or second later. As soon as the doorbell rang, she rushed out the door nervously to welcome him.

"I'm sorry Maverick, would you like to come inside for a drink?"

"No, no problem... it's great to see that you were all set to go. I arrived early because I assumed that I would have to wait on you. It was an even more surprise to have you rush me out the door. Are you sure, you weren't expecting someone else?

"No, don't be silly, Maverick. I didn't know where we were going so... I just threw on something."

She looked gracefully at him as he stood in his fitted blue jeans and his white silk shirt.

"You look beautiful."

"I thought we would go see a movie." He opened the car door.

"A movie sounds great. I plan to move to Washington, DC, soon," she told.

"When will you be leaving?"

"Not soon enough — probably not until the end of the summer. I have to wait until my mother comes home from the hospital. I want to make certain that she is okay before I leave."

"I hope every thing is okay with your mother... why is she in the hospital?"

"She has sclerosis of the liver."

"That's thoughtful of you to wait until your mother comes home from the hospital, before you leave. Why are you going to Washington?"

"That's where all of my sisters live. Besides, my sister, Ginger said that I could come to live with her. I don't plan on staying here in Rocking Barrel for the rest of my life."

"I go to Washington all the time. I have a cousin there. Would you like for me to take you?"

"Sure, I would love to ride with you, that's after my mother gets better — of course."

After leaving the movies, Maverick drove Kim down to the lake where they parked and talked for hours. They kissed in between conversations, heating the windows with their emotions. Maverick drove Kim home and they said goodnight.

Although Joyce was released from the hospital at the end of the summer, Kim knew that she couldn't leave until she had fully recovered. Feeling stuck there, Kim enrolled herself in the community college.

"Why have you decided to come to this college? Your SAT scores are so high... you could attend any college of your choice. Any in the U.S.," the Dean told Kim that morning.

"Well, my family doesn't have the money and my mother is really ill. I just want to stay here until she gets better," Kim told.

Unfortunately, Joyce began to drink again and ended back up in the hospital by the end of October. Once again, Kim was stuck. There was no way that she could leave Rocking Barrel with her mother much more ill than before.

She was released from the hospital three days before Thanksgiving. Kim was once again delighted that she was coming home and looked forward to her recovery.

"Kim I guess you will be cooking Thanksgiving dinner. I'll supervise you in the kitchen of course."

"I should be able to handle that, as many times as I have helped you out in the kitchen. That's if you tell me how to make your famous stuffing. You'll probably have to coach me on seasoning the meats too."

That evening Ginger and the other Tucker girls called to say that they would be coming home on Thanksgiving morning.

"I'm going to sit up out in the living room for a couple of hours today. If I can get up and walk around a little tomorrow then I'm sure that I will be able to assist you in the kitchen to instruct you on making supper," Joyce said.

There was no way that Kim would pull off cooking Thanksgiving dinner without her mother's guidance. That following morning she helped her mother out of her bed and she sat out in the living room. They sat down and watched a couple of movies. Walking her mother back and forth down the hallway, Kim insured that she received her therapy. Joyce's Determination to get well pleased Kim substantially.

Kim was a little nervous about cooking Thanksgiving Supper considering that Joyce's cooking was a hard act to follow. She was quite surprised to find Joyce sitting at the kitchen table When she entered the room.

"Good morning, so are you ready to get started?" an energetic Joyce asked at six-o'clock that Thanksgiving morning.

"Yes," Kim said. She smiled nervously as her mother began to give her systematic instructions on preparing the stuffing for the turkey. She told her how to baste the ham and Kim prepared the potato salad. Cleaning the collard greens in the sink was the worst but by ten-o'clock that morning, everything was in the oven or on top of the stove cooking. She had even mastered the turkey in which George had let soak overnight in the sink after filling the water with salt.

"I'm getting a bit tired now Kim. I'm going to go in my bedroom to lie down. There's not much left to do... except for to prepare the pies and cakes. I'm sure that you can handle that without my help. Oh, don't forget to prepare the side vegetable dish," Joyce said, breathless.

She went into her bedroom.

After Joyce went to bed Kim began to prepare her pies, cakes and Joyce's favorite vegetable dish. These were all the things that Kim would normally prepare herself while her mother prepared the other items. In anticipation of her own collapse, Kim continued cooking until about one-o'clock that afternoon. Exhausted, she too went to take a nap to get ready for her big day.

239

Having entered the room, Little-Joyce asked, "Kim What are you doing sleeping this time of the day?

"Hey, when did you guys get here?" Kim awakened to find Mona, Ginger, Rosetta, Little-Ray, Sassy and Jasper standing next to her bed.

"We got in about an hour ago. Wake-up, we're getting ready to eat," Ginger said.

"What time is it?

"Three-o'clock."

"Jasper and Little-Ray, you guys wash your hands and come in to supper."

Kim washed her face to get a fresh start and joined everyone at the table. George said the blessing and carved the turkey and ham. Everyone was quite anxious to consume the meal in which Kim had prepared with her mothers instructions. Felicia even joined in at the table for the festivities. She sat quietly at the table, between Borne and Nicholas. Victor, Bobby and Calvin were not in attendance as usual.

"Mommy, we are all glad to see that you are doing much better now," Sassy said. She smiled with delight at Joyce, whose face glowed as she sat along side her seven daughters, two sons and two grandsons.

"You gave us quite a scare," Rosetta added as they sat their making trivial conversation. After supper, Rosetta, Sassy, Joyce, Mona and Ginger retreated to the bedrooms where they rested. Kim, Little-Joyce and Felicia cleaned the dishes.

Later that night after the girls were well rested, Ginger, Mona, Kim and Little-Joyce rode out to visit with some old high school friends. Feeling rather delightful after having several drinks along the way, the girls sat out in the car reminiscing. They talked about their childhood together and each retold stories as they recalled each occurrence. Kim sat listening quietly.

"What is bothering you, Kim? You've been rather subdued tonight. You have hardly said three words since we arrived to town," Little-Joyce said. Kim's nonchalant attitude now generated the interest of her older sisters.

"I can't believe that you guys did this to me!"

"Did what to you?" Ginger asked.

"You left me here alone, isolated with Felicia. You know that you didn't want to deal with her insanity, so you just brought her here and left her. You knew that she needed some psychological help! She's crazy! Now you show up two years later, as if everything is wonderful. Well it's not wonderful! I have had to deal with her torture and madness," she stated with

241

frustration and anger that evening. "I lay in my bed every night, fearful for my life because of Felicia. Everyone else in the house remain locked away safely in their room and sheltered away from her evil wrath! Meanwhile you guys remain hardheartedly unaffected in your cozy homes in Washington. No one seems to care what I am going through! I feel trapped in bondage here in Felicia's hellhole constrained by the same evil spirits, which bind her. Not to mention that I was raped last year, or do you know that already."

Kim drenched her sisters in her pity of her belief that they had deserted her in her time of despair.

"Yes Kim, we heard that you were raped. At least they got the bastard."

"Got him... no one got him! He is still walking around a free man. He has probably done or is doing the same thing to someone else as we speak!"

"Daddy said that you all went to court and that the guy was arrested."

"We did go to court and yes, he was arrested, however, the charges were dropped."

"Oh, we didn't know that."

"Well, we all have gone out with a guy who has tried to

force himself on us," Little-Joyce said as if this would some how ease Kim's pain.

"It was not like that! In those cases you can say no and nine times out of ten the guy will feel bad and let you go home. He usually backs off and listens to you. This was a violent rape. I didn't know this guy and he was much older than me."

"Well, you are okay now."

"Barely."

"Can I please come up there to stay with you guys? I can't take it here anymore."

"I told you that you could come," Ginger said.

"I can't come until mother gets better, perhaps by January."

Kim calmed herself, feeling somewhat relieved after speaking with her sisters.

They went into the house and settled into their beds. It was like old times. Everyone gathered at the breakfast table laughing and giggled the following morning. They spent the entire day watching television and updating each other on their corporate careers. The following morning, the girls left and were headed back home to Washington.

Chapter 20

Kim was depressed after her sisters left. She hadn't heard back from Maverick in months and thought that maybe he had forgotten about her. At least she did until that February morning when she received a telephone call from him.

"Hi Kim. I promised you that I would call when I was on my way to Washington."

"So are you ready to go? I'll be leaving on next Friday."

"Yes, I'm ready. I'll call my sister and let her know that we will be coming."

"Okay, I'll pick you up around ten-o'clock in the morning," he said.

Kim was relieved that he had remembered to call her. She called Ginger once again to tell her that she would be leaving that following Friday. She was so excited that she began to pack immediately. She was more than ready to go.

Kim was concerned when Maverick didn't arrive on time. She paced back and forth as she waited his arrive. As she stood there, she turned towards her house to break away from the harsh winter wind that blew violently against her face. Looking over at the front porch Kim noticed that her suitcases remain lain there.

244

She also noticed Joyce standing quietly behind the dark colored screen watching her every move but never saying a word. She stood in her pink and yellow flowered flannel nightgown smoking her cigarette. Even through the darkness of the screen, Kim could clearly see the sadness in her mother's eyes. This was the sadness that she displayed the night before when Kim informed her that she would be leaving for Washington.

She recalled the conversation that she and her mother had the prior evening.

"What are you going to do in Washington, DC?" she asked Kim.

"I'm going to get a job."

"Get a job doing what?"

"I don't know... as a receptionist, or typing perhaps."

"So when is Ginger coming to get you?"

"She's not coming to get me. Maverick is going to drive me in the morning."

"Well, if that's what you want to do then I guess I can't stop you," Joyce stated with tears in her eyes.

Wanting desperately to ease her mother's hurt, Kim contemplated staying at home. Even though she knew that she

245

had to leave that town. She strongly knew that if she stayed there with Felicia that her life would deteriorate. She watched her mother, vividly in her mind and imagined her moving all of her belongings back into the house. Reality reassembled and Kim regained her composure realizing that her possessions remained untouched.

To her relief, Maverick was now driving up in the driveway. They began to put Kim's belongings in the trunk of his car and as they had finally placed the last bit into his car, Ricardo drove up. He blocked Maverick's car in the driveway.

"What do you think you are doing, Kim," he said as he jumped out of the car.

He began to pull Kim's suitcases out of the car.

"Who are you and what do you think you're doing?"

"What does it look like I'm doing? You're not going anywhere, Kim!"

"Who is this guy, Kim?

"Maverick, this is my ex-boyfriend, Ricardo.

"Ricardo, what are you doing here? I'm leaving this evil town and moving to Washington, DC."

Yeah, so I heard! You're not leaving, not with him!" Tears

rolled down his face as he forcefully removed the remainder of Kim's bags.

"Maverick, I'm sorry... you can go ahead and leave. I'm so sorry for all this drama and thank you for offering to give me a ride," Kim said.

"Are you sure?"

"Yes, I'm sure... I'll see you later. Drive carefully," she said as Maverick got in his car.

He drove away down the street.

"I can't believe that you were actually going to leave town and not say a word to me! Not even good-bye," Ricardo said appearing judgmental.

"What are you doing here anyway?"

"Your mother telephoned me last night and told me that you were planning to leave town this morning."

"She did what?" Kim walked back into the house to question her mother's actions.

"Mommy, why did you call him?"

"You know that he loves you very much, Kim. How do you think it would have made him feel, to come here and find that you had left town? He would have been really hurt and you just don't do things like that to the people you love," she strongly advised.

She now wondered was it Ricardo that Joyce was waiting on... "Well, if he loved me so much, then why didn't he come to see me during the time that you were away in the hospital?"

"You know I love you, Kim. If you had answered my telephone calls, I would have come by to see you. If you want to go to Washington, then we can go together. You should have come to me and talked to me. I would have taken you there. You know that my sister, Kara, lives there."

"I guess I was meant to be stuck here in Rocking Barrel," Kim said.

"You don't have to be stuck here. Like I said, we can go together but we have to plan it out. You can't just jump up and leave like that," Ricardo said.

"Why not, I'll never get out of here if I keep procrastinating."

"I tell you what. Will go up there and stay for a couple of weeks... to see if we can find us some jobs. We don't want to just put ourselves out on our family."

"That's right," Joyce agreed.

"My sister said that I could come. Why do I have to wait? I know that I can find a job," Kim said. Ricardo got on the telephone and called Kara, who agreed to let him come to stay with her.

"Kara said that I could come too... grab your things and we are on our way," Ricardo said.

"Are you serious? Yes, come on," he said.

He grabbed three of her bags. Although Joyce was distraught that Kim was still leaving town she seemed more at ease now that Ricardo would be the one taking her.

"Mom I guess this is Good-bye. I'll call you as soon as we get there," Kim said.

With her eyes full of tears Joyce gave Kim a big hug and said... "You be a good girl Kim."

Kim and Ricardo rushed over to his house to pack his clothes. Mrs. Durkin, Ricardo's mother, was waiting at the door when they arrived.

"Kara called to say that you were coming there to stay," she said.

"Yes, Kim and I are leaving today."

"Kara didn't say anything about Kim."

"Kim will be staying with her sister."

"You're leaving today?"

"Yes, as soon as I can get packed," he informed.

In less than an hour Ricardo had gathered his possessions and the two of them were on their way to Washington, DC.

As Ricardo drove out onto the highway a relaxing feeling came over Kim. She felt calm knowing that Ricardo was joining her and knowing that she wouldn't be alone.

"I am so glad that we have gotten out of Rocking Barrel," Kim said.

A vibrant smile appears upon her face as a sensation of absolute peace and serenity satiate within her growing with each hour as he drives away. The heavy weights of the evil crows, in which Felicia insisted and Kim certainly believe, which rest upon her shoulders appear to drift slowly away with each mile.

As they entered Washington, DC, Kim noticed the clear clouds, which flourish roundabout her. She appreciate the atmosphere which although smug — far more vibrant than the desiccate and eerie skies which surround Rocking Barrel. Tears of contentment filled her eyes as she found it hard to believe that she had finally gotten away from Felicia and that dreadful town. She was finally there and she knew that there was no way that she would return to Rocking Barrel.

Kim had no idea that cold winter afternoon having arrived there in Washington of the changes that would take place in she and Ricardo's lives. He had driven more than four hundred miles for them to make a new start and they both believed that their departure from Rocking Barrel would bring about a breathtaking change in their relationship. Kim and Ricardo had never been as content as they were that afternoon.

Kim felt that she was ready for the workforce and was looking forward to joining her five sisters. Their lives as they had once known it seemed far, far behind them now as they made promises of never going back.

As she sat there in the car in front of Ginger's apartment waiting for her to arrive home from work, she thought profoundly back to the day that she and Ricardo stood on the River Bank.

In their deepest desperation they wanted out of Rocking Barrel and its tight bear hug which appear to pull them underneath to its bottomless pit. Kim and Ricardo sat there on the riverbank the majority of the day drinking cheap white-liquor and cuddling endlessly. They remained there throughout the day into the early evening. They watched the stars struggle their way through the thick clouds to make their appearance into the night.

"If I jump in, would you follow me? Look at those clouds... they look like they could just grab us and never let go," Kim said after they finished drinking the liquor.

"What are you talking about now Kim?"

"Look at the clouds. Why are the clouds in Rocking Barrel

always so dark and gloomy? Do you think they're like that everywhere in the world? I'm certain they're not... it's just another part of Rocking Barrel's curse I imagine," she said.

She kissed him on his lips.

"I don't know what you're talking about, Kim" Ricardo replied.

"Well, would you?"

"Would I what?"

"Would you jump?" Kim asked once again moving towards one of the steep rocks as if to jump.

Ricardo grabbed her arm pulling her back towards him and away from the river's bank.

"What is wrong with you Kim? Are you crazy?"

"Maybe, I don't know. All I know is that if I don't get out of this God forsaken town, I will go crazy," she promised.

"I promise you that I'll get you out of here. I don't know what I would do if I lost you. We'll look back on this day one day and laugh."

Ricardo finally awoke. He kissed Kim softly on her lips and held her tightly in his arms. The two of them now look up at the bright lights there in Washington. Ricardo began to laugh hysterically.

"What's so funny?"

"I told you that we would get out of there," he said. It was as if he had read her mind, with those words, Kim was certain that everything would be blissful for them in Washington. She hadn't heard Ricardo laugh like that for Several months. She joined him in his laughter. Minutes later Ginger arrived home.

"Hey Ginger... we made it," Kim said.

"Let me open the door so that you can bring your things inside," Ginger said.

"Hello Ricardo. What are you doing here?"

"I drove Kim up," he said.

Ginger and Ricardo had graduated from high school together in Rocking Barrel. She had no idea at the time that the two of them were dating.

"Give me a minute Kim and I'll help you get your bags out the car."

"No, Ginger you relax. Ricardo and I can manage."

"Here's the key... take it with you. The door will lock automatically behind me."

Kim took the key and she and Ricardo went back out to the car to get her things.

"Kim I'm going to go to my sister's house now. She should be home from work," Ricardo said. They were done unpacking her things.

"Call me when you get there."

"Okay, I will."

Ricardo gave her a small kiss before leaving.

"So... are you two dating?"

"Yes, we've been dating for two years now," Kim told.

"I've always liked Ricardo. He's a nice guy."

Ricardo called when he got to his sisters house and once again before he went to bed. Kim and Ginger sat up talking most of the night, even though Ginger had to be the work at eight o'clock the following morning.

Kim was certain that everything would be heavenly there in Washington. She was finally there with her sisters and she and Ginger were getting along wonderfully. There was no way that she would ever return to Rocking Barrel.

ABOUT THE AUTHOR

Full of mystery and spirituality, Shadows of the Mind. Pam Randall allows me to be me — when writing, therefore — I prefer to be her. I live with my husband and have a daughter, stepson and grandson. I work in an Information Technology environment and live in North Carolina.